"I want to get you closure. I really want to find Lexi and her killer."

"I told you—"

He pressed his fingers over her lips. Then his eyes—those eerie pale brown eyes—darkened as his pupils dilated. His fingers slid across her mouth...caressingly.

He jerked his hand away from her mouth. "I know who you think killed your sister. I know."

And she waited for him to refute her belief as he always had. But he stayed silent again.

"You're not telling me I'm wrong this time," she said.

He emitted a weary-sounding sigh. "I'm not as cocky as I was six years ago."

He was different. No less serious or determined or driven, but perhaps a little less confident. Lexi's case had shaken his confidence.

And maybe it had him second-guessing himself.

Because now he uttered the question she'd been waiting for him to ask since she'd overheard his confrontation with the reporters.

"Is he my son, Becca?" he asked. "Is Alex mine?"

THE AGENT'S REDEMPTION

LISA CHILDS

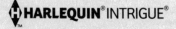

With great appreciation for my sisters,
Jackie Lewakowski, Phyllis Elsbrie & Helen Glover

ISBN-13: 978-0-373-74918-8

The Agent's Redemption

Copyright © 2015 by Lisa Childs

Recycling programs
for this product may
not exist in your area.

Printed in U.S.A.

Lisa Childs writes paranormal and contemporary romance for Harlequin. She lives on thirty acres in Michigan with her two daughters, a talkative Siamese and a long-haired Chihuahua who thinks she's a rottweiler. Lisa loves hearing from readers, who can contact her through her website, lisachilds.com, or snail-mail address, PO Box 139, Marne, MI 49435.

Books by Lisa Childs

Harlequin Intrigue

Special Agents at the Altar

The Pregnant Witness
Agent Undercover
Agent to the Rescue
The Agent's Redemption

Shotgun Weddings

Groom Under Fire
Explosive Engagement
Bridegroom Bodyguard

Visit the Author Profile page at Harlequin.com for more titles.

CAST OF CHARACTERS

Special Agent Jared Bell—The FBI profiler has had only one serial killer elude him, but that killer has hurt more than Jared's career—he's threatening the woman Jared loves.

Rebecca Drummond—She lost her sister six years ago to the Bride Butcher serial killer and she'll do anything to stop him from killing again—even put herself in danger.

Alex Drummond—Rebecca's six-year-old son could be in danger, too.

Lexi Drummond—The young bride disappeared six years ago from her last fitting for her wedding gown. Although her body was never found, she had lost too much blood to have survived.

Kyle Smith—The reporter has launched his career covering the Bride Butcher serial killer. But how does he know so much about the killer?

Harris Mowery—Lexi's abusive fiancé is Rebecca's number-one suspect in her sister's murder, but he has an alibi Jared couldn't break.

Amy Wilcox—The young bride's disappearance compels Jared to check himself out of the hospital against doctor's orders. Maybe that concussion is why he goes to Rebecca for help finding the bride.

Troy Kotlarz—Amy Wilcox's fiancé might not be too upset that she's gone.

George Droski—Lexi's male best friend had always been in love with her, but she never returned his feelings. Maybe he didn't want anyone else to have her if he couldn't.

The Bride Butcher serial killer—The killer can't resist Rebecca as bait.

Chapter One

Bulbs flashed, and Jared Bell flinched with each bright light as he ran the gauntlet of reporters with their microphones and cameras. "Special Agent Bell!" they called out to him as he walked past where they had lined up along the residential street. "Special Agent Bell!"

He ignored them or at least he tried to ignore them as he ducked under the crime scene tape across the end of a driveway.

"Have you found her body yet?" a reporter hurled the question at him. Even though Jared wasn't looking at the guy, he recognized the artificially deep voice of Kyle Smith, and he wasn't surprised Smith had showed up. This narcissist didn't just report the news; he tried to make himself part of the story—at least of this story, this case. He was as relentless as he was insensitive.

Jared flinched at the question, hating how it would hurt whatever member of the missing girl's family might have heard the question or would hear it on a later news broadcast.

They were anxiously awaiting news—any news—of their missing loved one. They didn't need to hear it like this—on the news. They needed to hear it from him directly—as soon as he learned something.

"Have you ever found Lexi Drummond's body?" another reporter yelled out the question. "It's been five years."

Six. Lexi had been the serial killer's first victim. And no, her body had never been found. Her family still waited for closure. But he had nothing to offer them. No body. No suspect. No clues…

If his head hadn't already been pounding from the concussion he'd sustained a few days ago, it would have started hurting then. Pain throbbed inside his skull where he could feel his heart beating—fast and frantically. As an FBI profiler, he had caught a lot of killers over the years—but not this one. Lexi Drummond's killer had eluded him and killed again and again and again.

Now the killer had taken another girl. Another victim…

Jared would find her, though. She would not become another Lexi Drummond. Not in any way. He had gotten way too involved in Lexi's case and way too involved with Lexi's family. He'd failed them and himself.

For the first time in his career, his profession-alism had slipped. But that had happened only that one time; he wouldn't let it happen again.

Jared ignored the reporters and flashed his shield to the officer posted outside the duplex. Then he slipped through the open front door. The girl hadn't been abducted from her home, but the police were searching it for any clues to who might have taken her.

Jared had to study all the aspects of the case in order to construct a profile of the killer. He studied the crime scenes, the evidence—if any—left behind, the manner in which the victim was killed, and he profiled the victim, too. He didn't believe this killer randomly chose his victims. So getting to know them better would help lead Jared back to their killer.

But hopefully Amy Wilcox was only miss-ing. Hopefully she wasn't dead yet—like all the other victims. Even though Lexi Drummond's body hadn't been found, too much of her blood had been discovered at the crime scene for her to have survived whatever wounds she had suf-fered. Six years had passed, but he could still see all that blood. So much blood…

He blinked away the memory of that horrific crime scene and focused on his current sur-roundings. Amy Wilcox's duplex was painted in fun colors—bright greens and yellows, like a highlighter that outlined the many picture frames hanging on the walls.

To get to know her better, Jared studied those pictures. There were photos of her water-skiing and rock climbing and running races. As athletic as she was, she wouldn't have been easy to abduct—which explained the signs of a struggle at the primary crime scene: the ransacked and blood-spattered dressing room from which she'd been abducted.

She had almost gotten away from her assailant there. Maybe she would get away from him again. Jared moved on to the next picture and froze, his whole body tensing.

She wasn't alone in this picture. She had her arm around another girl who was laughing into the camera with her. Unlike Amy who had dark hair and eyes, this woman was blond with sparkling blue eyes and a dimple in her right cheek when she smiled.

Lexi Drummond…

HER HAND SHAKING, Rebecca Drummond pushed hard on the off button of the remote. The TV screen flickered before going black but not before she saw *his* face again. Special Agent Jared Bell. With his reddish-brown hair and light brown eyes, he was still handsome—maybe even more handsome than he'd been six years ago because his features were more defined, more rugged. Dark circles rimmed his eyes and faint bruises darkened one side of his face.

The reporter's words rang in her ears: "FBI profiler Jared Bell checked himself out of the hospital against doctor's orders in order to take over the investigation into the disappearance of Amy Wilcox, which confirms speculation that she is the latest victim of the Bride Butcher serial killer."

Horror gripped Rebecca, paralyzing her. She wanted to run, but she couldn't move from the couch where she was sitting. She could only think of… Jared.

He had been in the hospital.

Why?

How badly had he been hurt that he had checked himself out *against* doctor's orders?

He was obviously still obsessed with the case. Obsessed with finding a killer that he already would have found had he listened to Rebecca.

But he had refused to listen to Rebecca about anything. Seeing him again should have brought back anger or pain or resentment. Instead, other feelings—so many other feelings—rushed over her, overwhelming her.

She grabbed a pillow from the couch and wrapped her arms around it, but she wanted to wrap them around herself—to hold herself together. The doorbell dinged, startling her into jumping and letting out a short cry of surprise.

The door shook as a fist pounded on it now. And a deep and familiar voice called out, "Are you all right?"

He'd heard her. She couldn't hide now, like she wanted to hide. She'd promised him that he would never see her again. She hadn't *fixated* on him because he was investigating her sister's disappearance. Her face heated as even now, all these years later, the embarrassment rushed back.

She had been a fool to think herself in love with Jared Bell. And she would be an even bigger fool to open the door and let him back into her life.

The door rattled harder. "I'm coming in!"

He would break it down; she had no doubt that he would, just like he'd broken down the walls of her grief and pain and opened her heart to him.

She had rebuilt those walls since she'd seen him last. She wouldn't let him back into her heart. But she had no choice about letting him into her life. She opened the door just as he was putting his shoulder to the wood, and he stumbled inside the living room.

He spared her a quick glance before visually searching the room for any threats. Even battered from whatever had sent him to the hospital, he was still in full protective FBI mode. He turned back to her and asked, "Are you all right?"

No. She hadn't been all right with seeing him

on her television—even though she had seen him on the news occasionally over the past six years. She certainly wasn't all right with him being in her house.

What if...

She shuddered to think of it—of *them* meeting. But that wouldn't happen. She would get rid of Jared quickly. She would make certain he was long gone before Alex came home.

She nodded and assured him, "I'm fine. The doorbell startled me because I wasn't expecting anyone." Not for an hour yet. "Especially not you."

His handsome face moved with a slight wince at her jab. But she knew that she hadn't really hurt him. He would have had to care for her to be able to hurt him.

"Why are you here, Jared?" she asked, and then reminded him, "You were the one who thought it best we didn't see each other anymore."

"I'm sorry," he said. "I didn't handle anything very well concerning your sister's case."

"My sister's case..." That was all Rebecca had been to him—just part of a case. She was the one who had foolishly thought they were more.

"Why are you here?" she asked again. "You didn't come here to apologize."

"I should have," he said, as if just realizing it himself.

The man was a genius. A real one. He had graduated high school at thirteen, college with a doctorate in criminal psychology at nineteen and then had been recruited into the FBI. He had worked many cases—solving them all—before he'd come up against her sister's killer. And lost...

Jared was a genius when it came to other people but he was completely oblivious when it came to himself.

She shrugged. "That was a long time ago." She wanted him to think she had moved on, but it felt like yesterday that she had lost him—so soon after tragically losing Lexi.

"I'm sorry," he said again, and the sincerity was there in the gruffness of his deep voice.

She didn't doubt that he was sorry, but she didn't care. She just wanted him gone.

"Why are you here?" she asked, impatience fraying her voice into sharpness. This was the tone that always—finally—got Alex's attention.

"Have you seen the news?" he asked. "Do you know about...?"

She grimly nodded as concern tightly gripped her heart. "There's another girl missing. She was abducted from the last fitting for her bridal gown."

It could only be one killer. Her sister's.

"I need your help," he said.

But he hadn't come to her when those other

women had been abducted. He hadn't needed her help then. Why was he asking for it now—when he hadn't listened to her six years ago?

"I already told you who killed Lexi."

He sighed—that long-suffering sigh that irritated her. Then he pulled a photo from a file he had clasped under his arm and held it out to her. "I need you to look at this."

She grimaced and backed away from him. The last thing she wanted to see was another crime scene. She already had one that she could not get out of her mind. "No."

"Please, Becca—"

"Don't call me that," she snapped at him. To Lexi, she'd been Becca. And to him…when she'd thought he actually cared about her.

But all Jared Bell cared about was his career—and how this one unsolved case could damage it.

"What should I call you?" he asked. "Ms. Drummond, or Mrs.…?"

"Rebecca," she said, refusing to reveal her marital status. It wouldn't matter to him anyway since it had nothing to do with the case.

"Rebecca," he repeated. "Please look at the picture."

She closed her eyes, and that old crime scene flashed through her mind: the wedding dress soaked with blood spilling out of the trunk of Lexi's car.

Her body hadn't been in the trunk. But it didn't matter. The coroner had confirmed she couldn't have lost that much blood and lived.

Lexi was forever gone.

"I need your help," he said again. "Please…"

She forced herself to open her eyes—to look. It wasn't a crime scene. But it might have been worse to see Lexi like she was in that old photo—alive with happiness—because it reminded Rebecca of how much she'd lost.

Just like seeing Jared again reminded her of how much she'd lost…

Panic pressed on her lungs, stealing her breath. "You need to leave," she said.

"Rebecca—"

She planted her palm against his chest. Even through his suit and shirt, she could feel the warmth of his skin and the hardness of his muscles. But she pushed him toward the door. "I can't help you—because you won't listen to me."

"Rebecca, I want to talk to you about Lexi—about how she knew this girl."

She shook her head. She couldn't look at the picture again—of her and the missing girl. "Ask Amy Wilcox's family."

His amber-colored eyes darkened with emotion. "I asked them." And from his grim expression, it hadn't gone well. "They had no idea that Amy had known Lexi."

She shook her head. "I had no idea, either."

"We need to compare their pasts," he said, "and find out where their paths might have crossed." Mercifully, he turned the photo over to the white back. But then he pointed to the date on it. "This was taken the month Lexi disappeared. That's too great a coincidence. We need to figure out their connection."

She shook her head again.

"Bec—Rebecca, I need your help," he implored her.

Heat arced between them as he stared at her. She avoided his intense gaze, averting hers. Then she noticed the clock on the wall behind his head, and her panic returned with even more intensity. She had no time to answer his questions. "You need to leave now!"

Before Alex came home—because if Jared saw him he would have more questions.

More questions she couldn't answer...

Chapter Two

Jared's heart pounded hard and fast beneath the warmth of her hand on his chest. He'd worried that she might slam the door in his face. After the mess he had made of everything, he wouldn't have blamed her if she had. But she'd let him in. Although after hearing her soft cry, he hadn't given her much choice. He would have kicked in the door to get to her—to make sure she was all right.

She was beautiful—even more so than she had been six years ago. Her blond hair was longer and lighter and her skin tanned as if she spent more time in the sun now. Of course six years ago she had been so focused on school—her first year of med school—that she'd no time for the sun or relaxation or her friends and family.

Until her sister had disappeared.

"You have to leave," she said as she shoved on his chest again.

Already light-headed from the concussion, he stumbled back a step. To steady himself, he reached out and clasped her shoulders. Her blue eyes widened as she stared up at him. The urge to pull her closer overwhelmed him. It had been so long since he had held her that he ached to hold her again.

But that wasn't why he had risked getting the door slammed in his face—or getting shoved out of her house. "There's a girl missing," he reminded her. "Her family is going crazy with fear."

They had gone even crazier when he'd asked them about Lexi Drummond. Amy's mother had gotten hysterical, hyperventilating so badly that they'd had to call for an ambulance. Her dad had been trying hard to hold his wife together even as he began to fall apart himself, shaking uncontrollably. Amy's fiancé was the only one who'd managed to voice their fears aloud. "He has her then—that sick bastard who kills brides. She's probably already dead!" And then the man, a big burly former college linebacker, had dropped to his knees and dissolved into broken sobs.

Jared released a ragged breath and repeated, "They're going crazy with fear." More so because of him, because he had taken away some of the hope they'd desperately been clinging to.

"Just like I went crazy," she murmured.

She hadn't gone crazy, but she'd certainly

been upset and vulnerable. And he would never forgive himself for taking advantage of that vulnerability—of her.

"You know what they're going through," he said.

"I can empathize," she said.

"You can help."

She shook her head. "I tried to help six years ago. I told you who killed Lexi, but you wouldn't listen to me."

"It's not him, Bec—Rebecca," he said. He wished it had been. But the guy had had an iron-clad alibi.

She sighed. "You wasted your time coming here," she said, "if you're still not going to listen to me."

"All I want is for you to look at the picture and tell me how Lexi knew Amy Wilcox." That was a lie. He wanted more—much more from Becca than that. But he had no right to expect or ask for anything from her—not even information.

She had barely looked at the picture. So he held it out to her again. But she had barely looked at him, either. Instead, she kept glancing over his head.

He was surprised to find her here—in Wisconsin and so close to where her sister's car had been found. He'd thought for sure she would have wound up in another state—maybe even in another country—for her medical residency.

Instead, she lived just down the road from the wooded area that law enforcement and search teams had torn apart looking for Lexi.

To no avail…

He glanced behind him, where she kept looking, and noticed the clock on the wall. Large metal hands moved across the surface of a barn picture, like a weather vane moving in the wind. Her house was cute—a sunshine-filled ranch with bright colors—like something that would've been featured in a country living magazine. He hadn't pictured Becca winding up living in the country.

She'd wanted to do her residency in a big city. A bigger life than the small town where she'd grown up—just like Lexi had wanted.

She tore her gaze from the clock to focus on the photo. But not him.

Couldn't she even stand to look at him? Had he hurt her that badly? Guilt clutched his heart, like her palm still clutched his chest. Instead of pushing him away, her hand held on to his coat and shirt—as if she needed some sort of support to look at the photo again.

"I've seen her face on the news," she said. "But that's the only place I remember seeing Amy Wilcox before."

"We can look into their pasts—see how they're connected. You can help me," he urged her.

She shook her head. "I don't know how she

knew Lexi. But then again I was gone so much—for college and med school—that I didn't know all of her friends. And Lexi was always making friends." She smiled wistfully—sadly. "Everybody wanted to be her friend."

Six years had passed, but it didn't appear that Becca's pain had lessened any. Her loss seemed as fresh and painful as it had when Lexi had first disappeared. She had loved her sister so much.

Regret clenched Jared's heart—regret that he had hurt her. And regret that his being here was hurting her again. He shouldn't have come. She wasn't the only one he could have asked about Lexi.

"Do your parents still have your sister's things?" he asked. He could talk to them instead. Maybe they would have something of Lexi's—her journals or photos—that would explain her connection to Amy Wilcox and maybe lead him to a suspect that they had both known.

Or at least the suspect had known both of them. Maybe they'd been unaware of him. Jared had apprehended many suspects whose victims had never officially met them. They hadn't even been aware that they were being followed.

"No," Becca replied shortly, dashing his hopes.

He cursed. But he wasn't surprised.

While some people kept shrines to their lost

loved ones, leaving their things exactly as that person had left them, others removed every trace of them—as if that could make them forget their loss and pain. Her parents had been so broken and devastated that they hadn't been able to talk to him or any of the other authorities. That was how he'd gotten so close to Becca—she had spoken for all of them, for her parents and for her missing sister.

"They couldn't handle any reminders of her," she said with a trace of resentment.

Had Becca been a reminder of her sister, too? Had they removed her from their lives, too? It might explain why she had settled in Wisconsin instead of the farm town where she'd grown up in Ohio—where her parents probably still lived unless that reminded them too much of Lexi, too.

"So I have her things," Becca said matter-of-factly. She wouldn't have wanted to forget her sister—no matter how much pain that loss caused her. She was incredibly strong; she had been strong six years ago—except for when she'd turned to him for comfort and support.

And oblivion. She'd told him she'd needed to think about something other than Lexi. Or actually that she'd needed to not think at all for a while. That was why she'd made love with him. He hadn't had any excuse—except that he had been weak—too weak to fight his overwhelming attraction to her.

The attraction he still felt for her. But he couldn't think about that. He couldn't think about how she'd felt in his arms, how sweet her lips had tasted. He had to focus instead on the case.

So he breathed a sigh of relief that all leads weren't lost. "That's great. We need to look through her stuff and find out how she knew Amy."

She stopped clutching his shirt and shoved at him again. Her voice cracking with panic, she said, "Not now. I don't have time. You have to leave. Now!"

Behind him, the door rattled and then flew open and a little blond-haired boy ran into the house. He stopped short when he saw Jared and stared up at him—his blue eyes wide with surprise. He asked, "Who are you?"

Your father. The words stuck in Rebecca's throat along with the scream of protest she had wanted to utter when the door had opened. Of course Tommy's mother would drop Alex off early today. The horn of the minivan tooted as Beverly backed out of the driveway.

"My name is Jared Bell," the FBI agent answered his son. "What's yours?"

"Alex…" Suddenly shy, the little boy ducked behind her legs and peered around her at Jared.

"Nice to meet you, Alex," Jared replied. Then he raised his gaze from the little boy and met hers.

She expected accusation or at least suspicion. But pain and regret flickered through his amber-colored eyes instead. "I understand," he said.

And her stomach clenched. Could he understand why she hadn't told him? She wasn't entirely sure that she understood herself. Of course his rejection had hurt her, and he'd told her that it would be better if they had no further contact. But he hadn't known that she was pregnant. She hadn't yet known she was pregnant when they'd broken up. But to break up, they would have actually had to be together. And all she had been to him was a slip in his professionalism. A mistake.

And she hadn't wanted her child to be a mistake to him, as well. So she'd chosen not to tell Jared. But occasionally guilt overwhelmed her— like whenever Alex had asked her about his father. And now, when father and son finally came face-to-face.

Jared continued, "I understand why you didn't want to talk about this *case*—with your son coming home."

Her sister had never been just a case to Rebecca. "Alex knows about his aunt Lexi," she said.

"I got my name from her," the little boy interjected as he peeked around her legs again.

Jared smiled at the boy. "It's a very good name, too."

And Rebecca's heart lurched at the deep grooves in his cheeks and at the warmth in his eyes. He was so handsome. But that wasn't the only reason for her reaction. She hadn't thought the no-nonsense FBI profiler would pay any attention to a child. He had never expressed any interest in them before. But he was being so sweet...

So Jared.

That was why she had fallen for him before—because he had been so sympathetic for her loss and so concerned for her well-being. She had thought he was falling for her, too. But he'd only been doing his job.

That was all he was doing now. She hadn't seen him in nearly six years. He had moved on to the next case—the next murder and the next killer. But he was back now—because there was another case.

Another missing woman...

Another family going through what she and her parents had gone through—what they were still going through. "I want to help you," she said.

He arched a brow as if surprised. "I thought you wanted to get rid of me."

She had—when she'd been worried that he would realize Alex was his son. But he didn't appear to have made the connection. Alex was small for his age, though. Perhaps Jared hadn't realized how old the little boy was.

She really didn't want to leave them alone while she retrieved the container of Lexi's pictures and journals. "Alex needs a bath before bedtime," she said. "He just got back from a playdate. Do you mind waiting?"

His body tensed with urgency. He probably hated waiting. Amy Wilcox had already been missing for days.

But Rebecca doubted that there was anything in Lexi's personal effects that could lead him to the young woman. If the same man who'd taken Lexi had taken Amy, then Rebecca already knew who he was.

But Jared refused to believe her. He believed an alibi instead. But the alibi could have been faked. Or a killer could have been hired.

"I'll wait," he said. And he was already pulling out his cell phone.

Of course he had calls to make. When she'd known him before, he had constantly been on his phone—following up leads, checking in with other agents. The man lived and breathed his job. When he had worked her sister's case, she had mistakenly believed his intensity had been personal.

But it was just who he was…

Intense.

Driven.

Determined.

But despite all those characteristics, he had been unable to find Lexi's body. Or Lexi's killer.

She left Jared to his calls and tugged Alex toward the bathroom. Usually after a playdate with Tommy, he was exhausted. When she hosted a playdate with the hyperactive Tommy, she was always exhausted afterward, too.

But now Alex was too curious to be tired. "Who is Jared Bell?" he asked as he pulled off his clothes and stepped into the bathtub.

Your father. The words popped into her head again but stuck in her throat. She couldn't tell either of them the truth. Not now.

But guilt settled heavily on her heart. She should tell the truth. She probably would have—had she not been devastated by Jared's rejection. But he hadn't just rejected her; he'd rejected what she'd felt for him.

He'd told her that she didn't really have any feelings for him. She was only fixated on him because he was investigating her sister's disappearance—that he had become a surrogate of Lexi to her.

For such a brilliant man, he'd been incredibly dense and insensitive.

"Mr. Bell is…" She had no idea what to tell her son. Jared had never really been a friend. And she couldn't tell Alex that he was an FBI agent. Her little boy would never go to sleep because he would have a million questions for Jared.

Alex was such a bright and inquisitive boy. His teachers had already moved him up a grade because they couldn't challenge him. With his blond hair and blue eyes, he looked like her, but he had his father's brilliance.

She'd had to work hard for her grades. That was why she'd been so consumed with studying that she'd lost touch with her sister. Then she'd lost her entirely.

"He has a gun, Mommy," the little boy said.

How had he noticed the weapon holstered beneath Jared's jacket?

"Was that why you hid behind my legs?" she asked. "Are you scared of him?"

Alex shook his head and sent droplets of water flying across the sand-colored tile walls and floor and her T-shirt. "No. He has a badge, too."

Jared had always worn his badge clipped to his belt, but his jacket covered it. Of course her observant little boy would have somehow noticed it. He missed nothing. But a father…

"Mr. Bell is an FBI agent," she reluctantly admitted.

As she'd expected, Alex sprang out of the bath, dripping water everywhere. "Can I talk to him? Can I?"

Before he could head to the door, she caught him up in a towel and dried him off and stalled.

"Do you think he'll let me touch his gun?" Alex asked. "Do you think he ever shot somebody with it?"

She was pretty certain that he had, but not the person she'd wanted him to shoot—the person she was certain had killed her sister.

"It's your bedtime," she reminded her son.

"Oh, Mom, I can go to bed anytime," Alex protested. "He's an FBI agent!"

"And he's here to talk to me about Aunt Lexi," she said. "But you'll be able to talk to him another time." After she gathered her courage and told them both the truth.

It was time. It was actually past time that Jared and Alex learned they were father and son.

"If I see him again," Alex muttered.

"You will," she promised. But would he? Even after she told Jared the truth, would he want anything to do with his son? Would he want to be a father?

Or was he still all about his career?

The little boy dragged his feet getting ready for bed. He took forever to get into his pajamas and brush his teeth. And when she finally settled him into his bed, he sprang right back up.

"Mommy, there's a man looking in the window!"

A creative child, he always came up with inventive excuses for not going to bed. So she was only humoring him when she turned toward the window. But then she saw the man, too, staring into her son's bedroom.

And she screamed.

Chapter Three

Her earlier soft cry had struck Jared like a blow. This one—loud and full of fear—pierced his soul. He ran down the hall she'd gone through and nearly collided with her as she rushed out of a room, the child clutched in her arms.

"Someone's creeping around outside," she said, "looking in the windows."

He drew his weapon from beneath his jacket and headed toward the door. "Lock it behind me," he directed her. "And don't unlock it for anyone but me."

He stepped outside and lights flashed and voices shouted. "Special Agent Bell! Special Agent Bell!"

He flinched at the lights and the noise and the fact that he hated reporters. He wanted to step back inside and slam the door shut on all of them. But he'd had Becca lock it behind him. If he knocked and had her open it, they would see her and take pictures and bombard her with intrusive, insensitive questions like they had when Lexi had disappeared.

Six years ago Becca had hated the reporters as much as he had. Actually more. He hadn't begun to hate them until they'd turned on him—highlighting his one failure instead of all his success in apprehending serial killers.

"You're all trespassing," he informed them. "If you don't get off this property, I will have the local authorities arrest you."

While some of the reporters knew him well enough to know that his threat wasn't empty and they began to walk away, another stepped forward—probably the one Becca had seen through her son's bedroom window since the man stepped around the side of the house.

"Your being here confirms that this place belongs to Lexi Drummond's sister," the reporter brazenly said.

"My presence confirms nothing," Jared replied. He holstered his gun, but then pulled out his cell phone. His threat wasn't idle; he intended to have them all arrested—especially this man.

This reporter was tall and thin with a thick head of mostly artificial-looking blond hair and a big, snide grin. He wasn't just doing his job; he enjoyed annoying the hell out of people, especially Jared.

The man—Kyle Smith—shrugged shoulders that Jared suspected were as fake as his hair—since they moved strangely beneath his suit jacket, like they were more padding than muscle and bone. "County tax records confirm this property belongs to Rebecca Drummond."

Jared breathed a silent sigh of relief. He had been pretty sure that the press hadn't followed him here. But with the concussion, he wasn't quite himself yet. Maybe he hadn't noticed someone—like Kyle Smith—tailing him.

But apparently they had just done the same research he'd done to find Rebecca Drummond. Or at least Kyle Smith had. Had he brought the others with him, like a pack of dogs, to attack?

Then Kyle attacked as he shoved the microphone in Jared's face and had his cameraman zoom in on him. "So is Rebecca Drummond's young son yours?"

It was probably a good thing that he'd holstered his gun, or he might have threatened the man with it. Instead, he punched in the number for the local authorities, identified himself and gave the address where he needed backup to disperse trespassers.

"No comment, Agent Bell?" Kyle said with a sneer.

He had no comment that he could make publicly without his supervisor reprimanding him. And there was no point to answering any of Kyle's questions. The man twisted Jared's replies to suit his own purposes.

Apparently, he wanted to expose all of Jared's mistakes. Getting involved with a victim's family member had definitely been a mistake. But that had been six years ago, and the boy had to be younger than that. Alex hadn't looked much older than the toddler Jared had recently been helping protect. His head pounded, reminding him of the concussion that had rewarded his efforts. According to the doctor, he was lucky to be alive and have his memory intact.

Not that he could have forgotten Becca. He doubted he would ever be able to forget her. During the past six years, she had never left his mind. He'd seen her beautiful face in his dreams and in his waking moments. He'd thought of her often, wondering how she was doing—hoping she'd been able to move on after the loss of her sister.

"You're not here to see your son?" Kyle prodded him with the question and that infuriatingly snide grin.

Jared fought the urge to glare at the man, too. Then, against his better judgment, he replied, "I'm investigating the disappearance of Amy Wilcox."

"And how can Rebecca Drummond help you with that?" Smith asked. "She's convinced her sister's fiancé killed Lexi despite his rock-solid alibi."

Jared wished she'd been right. But the alibi

was indisputable and Becca's judgment seriously biased where her almost-brother-in-law was concerned.

Sirens wailed in the distance as Jared's backup approached. "Whoever is still on this property when the local authorities arrive will be arrested."

"You've let a serial killer run free for six years, Special Agent Bell," Kyle taunted him, "but you would arrest some reporters just doing their job?"

"You're not just doing your job." Jared had gotten that impression from the reporter before—that this was personal. Had Jared put away someone he'd known and cared about? Did the guy have some kind of vendetta against him? Why else would the reporter go after him like he did?

To suggest that Becca's son was his...

It was preposterous. To think that he was a father, that he had been a father for six years and had never known...

His heart lurched in his chest as he considered the possibility that he had son.

No. It wasn't a possibility.

HER NERVES FRAYED, Rebecca waited for Jared to ask. She'd heard the reporter's speculation—the one who'd been looking through Alex's bedroom window. That man had wondered if Alex was Jared's son.

Why hadn't Jared?

Fortunately Alex hadn't heard any of the reporter's questions or comments. She had tucked him back into his bed and drawn the blinds. And, despite the excitement, he had fallen asleep. She probably needed to thank Tommy for that. If his playdate friend hadn't worn him out, there was no way Alex would have fallen asleep after catching a man looking in his window. Or with an FBI agent in the house.

Or maybe it was because of the FBI agent that he fell asleep—because he felt safe. Was that because Jared was FBI or because Alex instinctively felt a connection with him?

It didn't matter that Alex hadn't heard the reporter's questions. He already had questions of his own. He'd already asked her who his father was.

He deserved an answer. He deserved a father. But Jared hadn't even wanted to be a boyfriend all those years ago. She couldn't imagine how he would have reacted if she'd told him she was pregnant. He probably would have thought she was trying to trap him because she was so fixated on him.

He was now focused on the contents of the plastic container in which Rebecca had preserved all of her sister's pictures, journals and letters. He kept flipping through the photos, flinching when he came across the ones of a bruised and battered Lexi.

"He did that to her," Rebecca said. But she hadn't known that until she'd found the pictures in Lexi's journal. Why hadn't her sister told her that her fiancé was abusing her? Because Rebecca had been too busy? Had Lexi thought she wouldn't care?

Lexi was only two years older than Rebecca, so they'd always been close growing up. When she'd graduated Lexi had stayed home and attended community college for a medical assistant program. Rebecca was the one who'd left home—for college and med school.

Guilt gripped Rebecca, squeezing her heart. Maybe if she had been more available to her sister, Lexi would have told her what was going on, and she could have helped her. She could have saved her...

Anger joined her guilt as she glanced at the photos, too. The man was a monster to have done that to sweet, beautiful Lexi.

"She took those photos as evidence against him," Rebecca said, "in case something ever happened to her." That was what Lexi had written on the journal pages between which those photos had been tucked. "She wanted *you* to know who her killer would be."

Rebecca waited for Jared to bring up that

damn ironclad alibi again. But the FBI profiler remained curiously silent and focused on those photographs.

Her pulse quickened. Was he beginning to believe her? To believe the evidence Lexi had left for him?

Of course Lexi hadn't known who would be investigating her case. But she'd known that she would die and that there would be someone investigating her death.

Poor Lexi...

If only she'd told Rebecca what was going on.

But Rebecca had been too busy studying. She'd been too busy for much more than a short texted reply to her sister's usual text, You still alive?

Yes, I'm still alive.

When she hadn't heard from Lexi in a while, she had texted her the question: You still alive?

Lexi had never answered that text.

Rebecca closed her eyes as the pain overwhelmed her, and tears threatened. It didn't feel like six years had passed since she'd lost her sister. It felt like yesterday.

"I'm sorry," Jared said.

"Why?" He had already apologized for how he'd handled the situation with her—the line he regretted crossing into her bed.

Images flashed through her mind—of the two of them in bed, of naked skin sliding over naked skin. Of his lips on hers as he kissed her with all his intensity focused solely on her. He had made love to her so thoroughly, so passionately that it was as if she could still feel his hands on her body, his lips on her...

Desire rushed through her, heating her. She didn't regret that he had crossed that line with her. She only regretted how it had ended. That he had ended it.

But she didn't want any more apologies from him. Not when she owed him one. She was the one who'd been keeping a secret from him for too many years.

"I'm sorry I came here," he explained, "and opened up all this pain for you again."

She chuckled at how he didn't understand her feelings any better than he had six years ago. "You think you just reopened it?"

He shrugged. "Maybe it wasn't me, but Amy Wilcox's disappearance had to have brought everything up again—all those feelings."

"She isn't the only victim since Lexi."

But Rebecca didn't need to remind him of that. She could see his frustration in the slight lines around his eyes and mouth. She could feel the tension in his body. He blamed himself, as much as the serial killer, for the loss of those other victims.

"No, she's not," he acknowledged, and the guilt was in the gruffness of his deep voice.

"But you never came here when those other victims first went missing," she said.

He held up the photo he'd brought with him—the photo of Amy Wilcox with Lexi. "I didn't find any connection between them and your sister."

"But their killer..."

"We don't have enough evidence to make that conclusion," he replied—uttering one of those patented FBI press release statements.

She nearly smiled. Maybe it was because he had been recruited so young into the Bureau that he was such a *company* man. Or maybe it was what she had concluded six years ago—all he cared about was his job.

"The media hasn't had any problem leaping to conclusions," she said. And not just about the murders but about her son's paternity.

But they weren't wrong about that. Had they been wrong about all the murders being the work of one killer?

"I didn't lead those reporters here," Jared assured her.

"I know."

While his specialty was profiling killers, he had made certain that he had all the skills of a field agent. He was an expert shot and defensive driver. That was why she'd been so excited when he had been assigned her sister's case—because she'd heard all the media praise about him.

But the media didn't praise him anymore—because he'd never found Lexi's killer. Or Lexi's body.

"The pain wasn't just *reopened*," she said. "It never *closed*."

He flinched again, like he had looking at the pictures of a brutalized Lexi. "I'm sorry you never got closure."

Everyone talked about needing closure. Needing a body to bury. Or a killer to curse.

"I'm not sure *closure* would make it hurt any less," she admitted. Lexi would still be dead.

He stepped closer to her, and his voice was low and gruff when he said, "I want to get you closure. I really want to find Lexi and her killer."

"I told you—"

He pressed his fingers over her lips. Then his eyes—those eerie, pale brown eyes—darkened as his pupils dilated. His fingers slid across her mouth…caressingly.

Her breath caught in her lungs, and her pulse quickened with awareness and desire. How could she want him again? She wasn't hurting over Lexi's loss alone. She was hurting over losing Jared, too.

He jerked his hand away from her mouth. "I know who you think killed your sister. I know."

And she waited for him to refute her belief like he always had. But he stayed silent again.

"You're not telling me I'm wrong this time," she said.

He emitted a weary-sounding sigh. "I'm not as cocky as I was six years ago."

He was different. No less serious or determined or driven but perhaps a little less confident. Lexi's case had shaken his confidence.

And maybe it had him second-guessing himself.

Because now he uttered the question she'd been waiting for him to ask since she'd overheard his confrontation with the reporters.

"Is he my son, Becca?" he asked. "Is Alex mine?"

Chapter Four

Jared's heart pounded fast and furiously as he waited for her answer. Or maybe because he'd touched her. He shouldn't have touched her. Because now he wanted to touch her again.

But if her son was his and she had never told him...

Could he ever forgive her? She had stolen almost six years of her son's life from him—years he couldn't get back. But her son couldn't be almost six years old. He was too small.

Like Jared had been for his age...

No. He shook his head in silent denial of his own thoughts and suspicions.

"I'm sorry," he said. "I have no business asking you that. I must've let Kyle Smith get inside my head." And of course the reporter had just been trying to get a reaction out of him— some scandalous footage to run over and over on his broadcast.

She blinked as her blue eyes widened with confusion. "Kyle Smith?"

"The reporter." Jared chuckled. "That egomaniac would hate that you don't know his name."

She glanced toward the black screen of her TV. "I try not to pay much attention to the news."

But since she'd known about Amy Wilcox's disappearance, he doubted that she was any more successful at ignoring the media than he was.

"I've been working on that myself." In his job, he had to know how to handle the media or he could tip off a suspect or undermine his own investigation. He lifted a hand toward his throbbing head. "Maybe I only let him get to me because of the concussion."

He wished he could blame the head injury. But he suspected that maybe it was wishful thinking instead…that Becca's son was his. He wanted a connection to her—something more than Lexi's unsolved murder to bind them together.

"How did you get the concussion?" she asked, her voice soft with concern.

After the way he'd treated her, how could she care about him at all? But that was just her nature, the reason she'd wanted to become a doctor, because she cared about people. All people. It was nothing personal. She'd had six years to realize that, although he hadn't been sensitive about her feelings, he'd been right. She hadn't really been in love with him.

"How did you get hurt?" she asked again, and now the concern was in her beautiful eyes as she studied his face, maybe trying to medically determine if he'd checked himself out too soon.

He shrugged off her concern and his own stupidity. "I didn't stick to just profiling."

"Do you ever?" she asked, and a twinkle flashed briefly in her blue eyes as if she was teasing him. Maybe she'd forgiven him for how he'd treated her.

"As a profiler, I do have to spend a lot of time out in the field," he said, "analyzing the crime scenes, the evidence, interviewing suspects, hopefully following leads to more suspects…"

"I know what you do," she reminded him.

Six years ago he'd kept her apprised of his investigation—probably too apprised. He'd told her when he'd interviewed her sister's fiancé. But she hadn't agreed with his findings. Even if the guy hadn't had an alibi, Jared truly hadn't felt like the man had killed his fiancée. Harris Mowery's shock and anger over Lexi's disappearance had seemed very genuine. But maybe Jared had been so cocky and overconfident back then that he hadn't read Harris as well as he'd thought he had.

"So what were you doing this time?" she asked. "That wasn't just profiling?"

"Protection duty."

She laughed. "You were playing bodyguard?"

He should have been offended. After all he wasn't the too-small-for-his-age child that he had once been. He was tall and muscular now, but he was no bodyguard. He'd learned all the skills of being a field agent, but protecting someone wasn't something he had done often enough to get good at it. Usually he came on the scene when it was too late for protection—when the victim had already gone missing or been found dead.

He rubbed his head where he'd taken the blow from the butt of a gun. He was lucky he hadn't been shot instead, but the killer hadn't wanted to forewarn his victim and have her get away again.

"I'm not a very good bodyguard," he admitted.

Her eyes widened with alarm. "Did whoever you were protecting get hurt?"

He breathed a sigh of relief. "No, but that was thanks to better agents."

She tilted her head, and a lock of blond hair fell across her cheek. He wanted to brush it back; he wanted to touch her again. He was close enough. He only had to lift his hand again, like he had touched her lips. His skin tingled yet from that too-brief contact.

Then she mused aloud, "You are different than you used to be."

A self-deprecating grin tugged at his mouth. "Less cocky than I used to be?"

She smiled, too. "Yes."

He didn't have to tell her why; she knew—because he'd failed to find Lexi's killer. He had failed all the subsequent victims of Lexi's killer, too. And most of all, he'd failed Becca.

He hadn't given her the closure she needed. She didn't seem to think it would help, but he'd seen it help others—when he'd found their loved ones' killers. He'd had a lot of success in his profiling career with the Bureau. He'd actually had mostly success and just this one failure when it mattered most.

Because Becca mattered most.

"I'm sorry," he said again. He couldn't apologize enough to her—for so many reasons.

"I wish you'd stop saying that," she murmured as she stepped back from him and lowered her gaze, as if she couldn't look at him.

He stepped closer, not wanting any distance between them. And he touched her, just his fingers on her chin, tipping her face up so that she met his gaze again. So that she would see his sincerity when he told her, "But I am...sorry. I'm sorry for how I treated you. And I'm sorry for not catching your sister's killer yet. And I'm sorry for letting Kyle Smith get to me so that I accused you of keeping my son from me."

She pulled away from his touch and lowered her gaze again. Maybe she wasn't willing to forgive his unfounded suspicion.

He groaned. "Right now I'm the most sorry about asking you if Alex is mine. I know you better than that. You would never do something—"

She lifted her hand and pressed her fingers to his lips, stilling them. "Jared..."

It was still there. The attraction. It had overwhelmed him six years ago, so that he'd acted on that attraction instead of his better judgment. If anything the attraction was even stronger now.

He lifted his hands to cup her shoulders, to pull her into his arms. But then his damn phone rang. He silently cursed the timing. But he couldn't *not* take the call. A young woman was missing.

He stepped back from Becca, so that her hand fell from his face. And he pulled out his cell phone. He recognized the number as belonging to another agent—an agent who had recently become a good friend. So it could have been a personal call. He could have ignored it and reached for Becca again.

But dread clenched his stomach into knots. And he knew...

Even before he clicked the talk button, he knew what special agent Dalton Reyes would tell him. A body had been found. He was no longer working a disappearance; he was working a murder.

"AGENT BELL HERE," he answered his cell.

But he wasn't there. Even though he stood only a couple of steps from Rebecca, he was already gone—already off to handle whatever had come up with this call.

Fear gripped Rebecca. She glanced down at the photo of Lexi and Amy Wilcox, smiling, with their arms around each other. She wished she'd known how they knew each other—what had connected them in the past. Because she had a horrible feeling they had another connection—that they were both dead—murdered by the same man.

But why would Harris have murdered Amy? Rebecca needed to go through her sister's things again and try to figure out how Lexi had known Amy and if Harris would have known her, too.

"I'll be there as soon as I can," Jared told whoever was on the phone. Then he clicked off the cell and slid it back into his pocket.

"Did they find her body?" she asked. Tears stung her eyes with sympathy for what the young woman's family would go through—for the loss and pain.

He lifted his shoulders, but it wasn't a shrug. "There's been no confirmation yet. I have to leave, though."

He was the one who would make the confirmation—the one who knew the case better than everyone else no matter how short a time he had been working it. He would have immersed himself in it. He had even risked seeing her again, although he'd had no idea how she might react, in order to investigate the connection between Amy Wilcox and Lexi.

Despite saying he had to leave, he stood in front of her yet—as if there was something he wanted to say or do before he left her. He lifted his hand to her face and skimmed his fingers across her cheek, brushing back a stray lock of hair.

Her breath caught in her throat, choking her—choking back the words she needed to say. The truth.

He leaned down a little—as if he intended to cover her mouth with his. To kiss her...

She wanted his kiss. Her pulse quickened in anticipation of his lips sliding over hers. And she closed her eyes.

But his mouth never touched hers. She opened her eyes to find that he'd moved. His head was no longer bowed toward hers. And he'd taken a step back.

He took another step. "I—I need to leave."

She nodded. "I understand."

Unfortunately, he probably had a body to identify. And then he would be caught up in the investigation. He might come back—to follow up on the connection with Lexi. Or he might be too busy to come back, so he would send another agent instead.

He took another step back, nearing the door. Then he turned and reached for the knob.

Maybe it was because his back was turned. Maybe it was because she wasn't sure if she would ever see him again, but she blurted out, "Alex is your son."

His hand tightened into a fist around the door-knob. She thought he was going to open the door and just walk out. But then he turned around and strode back to her, and his gaze pierced her heart with its intensity.

Her chest ached as her heart hammered with fear and guilt. She expected an outburst. Angry words. Accusations. At least questions.

He had to have so many questions.

Answers jumbled together in her mind.

You said we shouldn't see each other again.

I didn't know if you would think I got pregnant to trap you.

I didn't know if you even wanted to be a father.

His mouth opened, but no words came out. Maybe his questions were as jumbled in his mind as her answers were in hers. Then he shook his head. In denial of her claim? Didn't he believe Alex was his son?

Maybe he thought she was trying to trap him even now. She had obviously wanted his kiss moments ago—moments before he'd walked away.

But a muscle twitched in his cheek. And those usually pale brown eyes had darkened with emotion. Then he turned away from her and walked back to the door. He didn't hesitate this time. He turned the knob and stepped out.

She tensed, bracing herself for the door to slam behind him. It closed with a soft click, but that click echoed throughout the living room with a finality that left her shaking.

Would he come back to ask any questions? Or did he not care that he had a son? Didn't he want to see Alex? To form a relationship—a bond—with his boy?

Nervous that her legs might give out, she dropped onto the sofa. What the hell had she just done?

He was on his way to identify a body—the body of a woman whose family was probably still holding out hope for her safe return. And then once Jared confirmed the identity, he would have to notify that family of their loss.

She couldn't have picked a worse moment to tell him the truth. He was in the middle of an investigation. And she knew how investigations consumed him.

"I'm sorry," she murmured. Not only had she not been fair to Jared but she hadn't been fair to Alex, either.

She should have told them both years ago. She

shouldn't have denied them the relationship they deserved to have. Why had she been so selfish?

Regret and guilt had tears stinging her eyes. But giving in to the tears would be selfish, too, and would accomplish nothing.

She would make it up to Alex. Somehow.

But she wasn't sure that Jared would ever give her the chance. She wasn't sure that he would ever forgive her.

The phone rang, shattering the silence of her living room. She grabbed up the cordless from the table next to the couch, so that the ringing wouldn't awaken Alex. She wouldn't even be able to look at her son now—not without guilt overwhelming her.

The number was blocked on the caller ID, so she hoped it wasn't a reporter. Maybe she should have just hit the off button. But she found herself saying, "Hello?"

And hoping it was Jared. Maybe he'd found his words. His questions. She would even welcome his accusations now.

She just wanted him to give her a chance to explain.

But there was only silence.

Maybe he hadn't found his words yet.

"Hello?" she said again.

A reporter would have talked, would have fired a million questions at her. It had to be him. He was probably just too mad to speak to her.

"Jared?"

"No, Becca," a male voice finally spoke. It was low and raspy, and she wasn't certain that she'd ever heard it before. But how did he know the nickname that only Lexi and Jared had ever called her?

"Who is this?" she asked.

The silence fell again, but there was no dial tone. He hadn't hung up. He was still there.

"Who is this?" she asked again, and goose bumps raised her skin as unease sent a chill running through her. She shouldn't entertain some crank caller. She began to lift the phone away from her ear to hang up.

Then he spoke again in that raspy, nearly unintelligible whisper. "You need to be careful…"

"Careful?" She didn't live a life of adventure. She lived a quiet life—focused on her son and her job.

"You need to be careful," the person spoke again—this time with more urgency.

"Why?" she asked.

"You're being watched."

She peered out the window. The sun was beginning to set, setting the window aglow with a yellow glare. She couldn't see anything but the yellow shimmer in the trees and across the grass. If someone was out there, she couldn't see them. Were the reporters staked out there somewhere?

Waiting to ambush her when she left for work in the morning?

"I know," she murmured. Those damn reporters.

They'd been relentless during the investigation into Lexi's case. They had followed her everywhere. And even after the case had gone cold, they'd checked in with her from time to time— wanting to interview her. Wanting to dredge up the tragedy and her pain...

"You don't know," the person said. "You don't know..."

She shivered at the ominous tone. "What don't I know?"

"That you're in danger."

The line clicked with the same finality with which the door had closed behind Jared. Then the dial tone peeled out.

Her hand trembling, she turned off the cordless and put it back down on the table beside the couch.

Why would she be in danger?

The serial killer only went after brides-to-be. She was not engaged. She wasn't even seeing anyone.

She was safe. Wasn't she?

Chapter Five

The silver car. The blood-soaked lace spilling out of the open trunk. Jared flashed back six years ago to finding Lexi's car. Unfortunately, Becca had been with him when they'd come across the abandoned silver Chevrolet.

There had been no body but so much blood…

Now there was a body…

No matter how many victims he had seen over the years, horror and dread still clutched at his heart. How could a human do this to another human? How could they act so viciously and subject another person to so much pain and cruelty?

He shuddered. And he wasn't the only one.

Special Agent Dalton Reyes's usually tanned complexion had gone ashen, and he shook slightly as he stepped back from the trunk. "That could have been Elizabeth…"

Dalton had recently found a woman in the trunk of a stolen car he'd run off the road. Fortunately, that woman hadn't been dead—just so injured that she had lost her memory.

"It wasn't," Jared said. "She's alive." And she had recovered her memory, as well.

Dalton expelled a ragged breath of relief. "She's alive, and she's amazing. I can't believe she agreed to marry me."

Jared glanced back over his shoulder and groaned. He'd taken a Bureau helicopter from the closest police post to Becca's house; that was how he'd made such good time—arriving while the sun was still up. How the hell had the media already gotten wind of their finding a crime scene?

News station vans rolled into the middle of the Indiana wheat field, kicking up dust that shimmered in the setting sun. Jared gestured at the local police officers. "Keep them back. I don't want any pictures of this scene leaking out."

Before he'd had time to notify the family. He turned back to the trunk. The victim's face was swollen and bruised but identifiable. It was Amy Wilcox. She stared up at him through open, glazed brown eyes; he only imagined the accusation in her gaze. The blame for not catching this killer before he'd killed again—before he'd killed her.

I'm sorry, Amy...

He'd kept apologizing to Becca, too. But now he knew why she'd been so reluctant to accept his apologies—because she owed him a bigger one.

Alex was his son.

His head began to pound, and he flinched. But he pushed the thoughts back. He couldn't afford to be distracted now. He'd deal later with the shock and anger that was rolling through him like those vans through the wheat field.

Now he had to get to Amy Wilcox's family— before the media did. But he wouldn't do that until he'd made certain that the coroner removed her body from the scene without the media getting any photos of her.

Where the hell was the coroner?

Was he or she lost? The media had no trouble finding the field.

"Did you hear me?" Dalton asked.

If the other agent had been talking, Jared hadn't heard him. Despite his best intentions, he was distracted—too damn distracted.

Becca had always distracted him but never more so than now—when he'd learned they had made a child together. He had a son...

"I'm sorry," he murmured. He'd been doing a lot of apologizing tonight. "What did you say?"

"Elizabeth agreed to marry me!" He slapped Jared's back. "I'm getting married—thanks to you!"

"Me?" He was shocked—not shocked like he'd been when Becca had told him he was Alex's dad. But he was surprised that Dalton would give him any gratitude for getting hit over the head.

Dalton grinned. His color was back now. And if a guy could glow, Dalton was glowing. "Elizabeth and I feel like you're part of the reason we're getting married. If you'd been the jerk I thought you were going to be and took the case from me, I wouldn't have fallen for Elizabeth. That's why I want you to be my best man."

"So you want me to be your best man because I'm not a jerk?" Jared shook his head. "I'm not so sure you're right about that. If I'd really thought that the Butcher was after Elizabeth, I would have taken the case." But he'd never really believed that the serial killer had grabbed Elizabeth—because she'd lived.

"You would have been right to take the case, then," Dalton agreed with a quick, regretful glance in the trunk. "So will you do it? Will you be my best man?"

"How can you think about that now?" Jared wondered.

Dalton glanced in the trunk again and shuddered. "I know my timing stinks, but I don't want to wait to marry Elizabeth."

"Do you see this?" Jared asked.

"Of course I see it."

"It's a message," Jared said. "He's mad that someone tried to blame the attempts on Elizabeth's life on him. He's making it clear what is his work and that women don't survive when he abducts them."

"He's a sick SOB," Dalton agreed. "But you know that."

"I know that he might try to get Elizabeth now—to prove that she wouldn't have survived if he'd actually grabbed her. You shouldn't get married now."

Dalton sighed. "You've never been in love, have you?"

Jared sucked in a sharp breath as if his friend had slugged him.

And Dalton apologized. "I'm sorry. I almost forgot about that first victim's sister..."

Jared had never been able to forget her. And now he never would. But he didn't want to talk about Becca. "I know you love Elizabeth, so you should want to keep her safe."

Dalton said, "I will keep her safe. And so will you. You're going to stop him."

"I've been trying for six years," he reminded his friend. "I haven't been successful yet." He hadn't even been able to establish a profile of the killer until the second victim. Since Lexi's body hadn't been found, he hadn't known exactly how this killer killed until then.

"You will be," Dalton said with absolute confidence.

The arrival of the coroner's van saved Jared from a reply. Six years ago he'd been confident he would stop this killer—like he'd stopped so many others before and after him. Now he wasn't so sure. But still, when he notified Amy's parents and fiancé, he found himself making them the same promise that he'd made Becca.

He would get this guy. For them. For Amy. For all those other victims. For Lexi. And, even though she had denied him six years of his son's life, for Becca. Maybe most of all for Becca.

He would stop this killer if it was the last thing he ever did.

REBECCA HADN'T MEANT to turn the television back on after Jared left. She really didn't want to see the news—not when she was sure that Jared had rushed out because a body had been found. Amy Wilcox's body.

The camera zoomed in on the open trunk of a silver car—and the blood-stained wedding gown spilling out of it. The scene in that fallow cornfield, so much like the one she and Jared had come upon, knocked her back six years. There had been so much blood…

But on the television screen, it wasn't just a dress that had been found, like it had been with Lexi. Moments later another camera followed a gurney on which lay a black plastic bag—a body zipped inside it—to the coroner's van.

The young woman had known Lexi—had

been her friend. And now both women were dead. Gone. Forever.

Was Jared forever gone? Or would he be back? He'd only been gone a few hours.

But he had been so shocked when he left. So betrayed.

He'd apologized for thinking that Alex could have been his, for thinking that she could have kept a secret like that. He had given her too much credit, and now she was the one who owed him the apology. So many apologies for all the years she'd kept him from their son.

She couldn't call him, though—even if she hadn't thrown away his phone number all those years ago. He was in the middle of what was now another murder investigation. He had a family to notify.

A killer to find...

Would he find him now? Would he look where she had been pointing him? Where Lexi had pointed her?

Had Harris known Amy Wilcox, too?

She turned off the television, shutting off the blond-haired man she realized now was Kyle Smith. Over the years he had hounded her more relentlessly than the others—wanting that follow-up interview, wanting to open up all her pain again. But he hadn't been interested in just Lexi. He'd wanted Rebecca to talk about FBI profiler Special Agent Bell, too. Like Jared, he hadn't wanted to talk about the real killer, either. Harris Mowery hadn't been newsworthy to him.

Maybe she could find what the FBI profiler and investigative reporter had failed to find—evidence leading to the real killer. She reached for the plastic tub of Lexi's photos and letters and journals and dragged it across the floor to the couch where she sat.

Rebecca had been so busy taking notes during class and studying that she'd had no time for journaling. But Lexi had written every night—sometimes just a short paragraph or sometimes pages. Remembering the date on the photo Jared had showed her, Rebecca reached for that year—the year that Lexi had disappeared. The journal cover was neon green with yellow and orange stripes. It was bright and happy like Lexi had always seemed. But inside those pages was another story—a dark story. This was the journal in which Rebecca had found those photos—of the battered and bruised Lexi.

Jared had been right: it was too great a coincidence that the women had been photographed together the month that Lexi had disappeared—especially when that woman later disappeared like Lexi had.

She had looked through this journal earlier when Jared had been there—after he had looked at it and determined that there was no mention of Amy Wilcox. The photos had distracted and angered her then. Now she focused on what Lexi had written. While there was no mention of Amy, Lexi had written several references to meeting someone she had nicknamed Root Beer. Amy's initials were the name brand of a popular root beer.

Could it be?

It was something Lexi would have done— something cute and funny. But they hadn't met that way. Lexi had met Root Beer at a support group for battered women.

Harris had been battering Lexi. Who had been battering Amy? From the news reports, Rebecca knew Amy's age; she was younger than Lexi. She must have only been in high school when she'd gone to those meetings.

So whoever had abused her was probably no longer in her life. From Lexi's comments, it was clear that Root Beer had impressed her with strength and wisdom beyond her years. Amy had actually been supportive to Lexi.

Could Harris have known?

Her pulse quickened as she skimmed over a passage. Then she read it again, aloud.

"Ran into Root Beer when I was out with Harris at the mall. She told him that she'd heard a lot of wonderful things about Harry. She said it, though, in such a way that he knew she had heard nothing wonderful about him. And he hates being called Harry. He got so mad at her sassiness that I thought he was going to hit her. But he controlled his temper until we got home and hit me instead. Root Beer saw the bruises at the next meeting and cried. It's not her fault, though. It's not even Harris's fault anymore. It's my fault for staying. But I'm even more afraid of what he'll do if I leave…"

That must have been why Harris had killed her—because she'd found the courage to leave him. Had he decided to kill Amy because he thought Lexi might have gotten some of that courage from the younger girl? But, in keeping with the other killings, he'd had to wait until Amy had gotten engaged—until she was ready to begin a happy new adventure.

Tears stung Rebecca's eyes. She blinked and wrinkled her nose, trying to hold back her tears. She had cried so many tears over the past six years. For Lexi. For herself. And for all the other victims.

Despite her efforts, she couldn't hold back her tears. Amy deserved them. But was she crying them for Amy? Or was she crying them for herself—out of guilt over not telling Jared he had a son?

She had spent the past six years trying to justify her action, or inaction, to herself. But there was no justification. Jared had deserved to know the truth and so had Alex. She had been so selfish, keeping her son—her amazing, intelligent, sweet son—all to herself.

Jared might never forgive her. Would Alex? Earlier she'd been confident that she could make it up to him. But she had spent the past six years trying to be both his mother and his father. And she'd failed.

She wasn't the male role model her son craved. She'd dated over the past six years, but she hadn't brought many of the dates around Alex. She hadn't wanted her son to get attached to any of them—because she hadn't been able to get attached herself.

None of them had been Jared, who was too smart. Too cocky. Too oblivious to her feelings…

Why hadn't she been able to get completely over him? She doubted he had thought that often of her over the past six years. But then she'd had Alex—precocious, brilliant Alex—to constantly remind her of Jared.

Heat flushed her face, and she quickly brushed away her tears—as if embarrassed that she'd been caught crying. She glanced to the hallway leading to the bedrooms and bath, but Alex wasn't standing there. He hadn't awakened.

She was alone.

Wasn't she?

Her skin prickled with awareness—of some-one's gaze on her.

You're being watched...

After that ominous call, she had closed the curtains. But with the lights on in the living room, someone could probably see through the thin fabric. Someone could be out there—watch-ing her.

Goose bumps rose along her arms, and she shivered. Not *could* be. Someone was definitely out there—watching her through the curtains. Why?

You're in danger...

And if she was in danger, so was Alex. After that call earlier, maybe she should have done more than close the curtains. Maybe she should have called the police.

And tell them what? That she got an omi-nous phone call? They couldn't investigate every prank call. And there had been no obvious threat made.

It had been more of a warning.

You're in danger...

Maybe she had let that call get to her—like Jared had thought he'd let the reporter get to him. Maybe that call had put her on edge, and she was only imagining that someone was watching her.

Gathering her courage, she turned toward the window and pulled back the curtain to peer out into the darkness. The light from the living room spilled out—and glinted off the eyes staring in the window at her.

She clasped her hand over her mouth to hold in the scream of sheer terror.

You're being watched...

It was no prank. Someone was out there.

You're in danger...

And whoever was out there meant her harm.

Chapter Six

Her beautiful face had paled to a deathly white, and her eyes had gone dark and wide with fear. Jared was furious with her for not telling him about his son, but he didn't want to see her like this—afraid of him.

"I didn't mean to scare you," he said. He also hadn't meant to come back to her house—especially after making the emotionally draining notification to Amy Wilcox's family. But something had drawn him back here—to her and their son. "I wasn't going to knock unless you were still up."

She stood in the doorway, trembling as she held open the door for him. The night air was cool, but he suspected she trembled over the fright he'd given her instead. He was tempted to take her into his arms, but she had her arms wrapped around herself, defensively—or protectively.

"That's why I looked in the window to see if

you were awake," he explained, "but I should have realized that after you caught Kyle Smith looking in…"

His son's bedroom window. The man was doing more than covering a story; he had crossed the line.

Becca shook her head even as her body continued to tremble. "That's not why I was so afraid."

"I didn't scare you?" Then what had frightened her? He peered around her and into the living room, but he saw no threat—nobody lurking inside with her.

"You surprised me," she said. And finally she stepped back, so that he could step inside the house with her. But she shivered again as she closed the door, shutting out the darkness.

Or maybe, despite the brightness of her living room, the darkness was already inside with her, spilling out of Lexi's open plastic tote of mementoes. Becca had been looking through her sister's things again. That was probably what had unsettled her so much.

"I'm surprised you came back," she said.

"You didn't think I would?" Was that why she hadn't told him about his son? She'd thought he wouldn't care—that he would want nothing to do with the boy. Maybe that was fair—since he'd once acted as though he'd wanted nothing to do with her—even though pushing her away was the hardest thing he'd ever done. Selfishly, he'd wanted to hold on to her.

But then she wouldn't have dealt with her grief and her loss. He hadn't thought she would heal if she continued to cling to him—to try to fill her emptiness with feelings for him. Feelings he had refused to believe were real.

He must have been right—or she would have told him when she'd learned she was pregnant. She would have let him be part of his son's life.

"I know you're busy," she said. "It was her?"

He nodded. Then he gestured at the open box. "Looks like you've been busy, too."

She expelled a shaky little breath that sounded as if she'd been crying. "It's too late to help Amy now, though. I shouldn't have tried to get rid of you when you first showed up at my door."

He knew now why she had. But he held back the words and his resentment because he could see from her slightly swollen and red eyes that she had been crying.

"I should have helped you right away," she said, and her voice cracked with emotion—with regret.

"Amy was already dead," he said. "She was probably dead before I even checked myself out of the hospital." Guilt twisted his stomach into a tight knot. "If I'd checked myself out sooner…"

But the coroner's preliminary exam had estimated that time of death had been around the time she'd been abducted. She had probably died in the struggle. Amy had fought for her life and lost.

Yet if Jared had caught the killer the first time he'd killed, Amy would be alive and so would all the other victims. But Lexi would still be gone.

Becca shook her head and admonished him. "You shouldn't have checked yourself out against doctor's orders."

"You would say that," he said, "because you're a doctor."

"No." She shook her head. "No, I'm not."

"But you were in med school…" When Lexi disappeared.

"I dropped out," she said.

"Because you were pregnant?" Had she given up her dream so she could carry his baby—to have his baby? Alone. She'd had no one to help her—if he was right that her parents had little to do with her because she was a painful reminder of Lexi.

She shrugged. "It would have taken me too many years of med school and residency and crazy hours to become the surgeon I thought I wanted to be."

"So what do you do?" How did she take care of their son? If she'd told him she was pregnant, he would have helped her. At least financially. He wasn't sure what he could offer her otherwise. He had always been so focused on his career that he'd never considered getting married and having kids. He'd never planned on being a father, so he wasn't sure he could actually be one.

"I condensed my crazy hours into a shorter time span by switching to a physician assistant program," she said. "I'm a PA at the local hospital."

"But you wanted to be a surgeon."

She shook her head. "Not after…not after seeing all that blood in the trunk of Lexi's car. I still see blood at the hospital. But I'm not the one cutting them open."

Like the Butcher cut open his victims…

She hadn't wanted to be anything like him—even if she would have been saving lives, instead of taking them like he did.

"I'm the one stitching them back up," she said with obvious pride and satisfaction.

The pressure in his chest eased slightly. She'd stayed in medicine. She hadn't completely discarded her dream. "That's good," he said.

She smiled. "I enjoy it. And I didn't have to go through all the crazy hours of a resident. I had more time for Alex." Her face flushed and she looked away from him.

So she probably missed his flinch of pain and regret. He'd had no time with Alex.

"Why did you come back?" she asked him.

"It's too late to wake Alex up now—if that's what you wanted to do."

He wasn't sure what he wanted. Or why he had come back. He'd been so angry with her—until he'd seen the fear on her face. Then he'd just wanted to hold her—to protect and comfort her. She still hadn't told him what had frightened her.

"It is late," he agreed as weariness overwhelmed him. Maybe he had checked himself out of the hospital too early, because he wasn't completely recovered. His head pounded from the concussion, and he didn't have his usual strength and energy. "Why are you up still?" He glanced down again at the open plastic tub. "What are you doing?"

Had she found something that had scared her?

"I read through Lexi's journal for the year that the picture of her and Amy was taken—"

"The year she disappeared," he interjected. It couldn't just be a coincidence. "I looked through that journal earlier and saw no mention of Amy's name."

"Neither did I," she said. "But Lexi liked to give nicknames to people she cared about. I think she gave Amy a nickname based on her initials."

She held out the journal to him, and he read the section she indicated. "Root Beer," he murmured.

Becca nodded.

"Her family didn't call her that."

"My parents didn't call me Becca—only Lexi did."

He had used it, too. He still thought of her as Becca. And he thought of her always.

"Lexi liked special nicknames," she said with a smile. But then her smile faded and she added, "She didn't have a nickname for Harris, though." She pointed to the section of the journal again, and her finger trembled. "He killed Amy, too."

If only it was that easy to find a killer.

He pointed out, "This isn't evidence of that."

"But it proves that he met her."

"It proves he met someone Lexi called Root Beer," he said. "We don't know that it was really Amy Wilcox."

She shook her head as if disgusted. "I should have known better than to think you would listen to me."

"I will investigate," he promised. "I will talk to Harris." He hadn't been able to find any connection between Harris and the other women who had disappeared. But he had a connection now—however tenuous—between him and Amy Wilcox. He could bring him in for questioning again.

But was he doing it to solve the case? Or just to make Becca happy? Since Harris hadn't killed Lexi, why would he have killed any of the other women—even Amy?

Becca breathed a sigh of relief. "Thank you." But the tension didn't ease from her body. She was still trembling slightly.

"If I didn't scare you earlier," he said, "what did?" And what still had her so on edge?

"I got a phone call shortly after you left—"

"One of those damn reporters?" They had all been staked out at the crime scene and the Wilcoxes' house. But one of them—probably Kyle Smith—could have called her from there.

She shook her head. "Not a reporter. I don't know who it was, but he called me Becca. And he warned me that someone's watching me— that I'm in danger."

Fear clutched his heart. "Why would someone tell you that? Why would someone want to scare you like that?" Unless it was true…

And if it was true, he couldn't take any chances. "I'm staying here," he said. "I'm staying with you until I can get protection duty on you and Alex."

"Isn't protection duty how you got your concussion?" she asked. But she didn't argue with him about staying. She opened a closet and pulled down a pillow and a blanket.

"I won't need that," he said. Because he wouldn't be sleeping. He'd nearly been killed the last time he'd done protection duty. But that wouldn't happen this time. He wouldn't drop his guard for a second—now that he was protecting his family.

THE RUMBLE OF a deep voice jerked Rebecca awake, her pulse racing. She wasn't afraid because she didn't recognize the voice but because she did. She'd heard that voice in her dreams before. How had she fallen asleep with Jared in her house?

But then she probably wouldn't have slept at all if he hadn't stayed. *You're being watched... you need to be careful...*

That ominous warning echoed in her mind. But with Jared watching over her and Alex, she'd felt safe. Until now.

Now she had that eerie feeling that she was being watched again. She glanced toward the door. She'd thought she had shut it, but it was cracked open now—wide enough that two pairs of eyes peered through at her. One gaze was the same blue as her own. The other gaze was the amber brown that haunted her dreams along with his deep voice.

"See," Alex said as he shoved open the door the rest of the way and ran into her room. "I told you she would be up. Mom never sleeps late."

"That's because you always wake me up." She reached out and caught her little boy, pulling him into bed with her. He squirmed and giggled as she tickled him.

Jared stared at their son now, his gaze full of longing. Then he looked at her, and resentment flashed in those amber eyes.

Guilt churned her empty stomach. She'd been so unfair to keep him from his son. But she hadn't known that he would want him. He hadn't wanted her; why would he want a child they had made together?

"Mom! Mom! Stop!" Alex protested. And his face reddened as if embarrassed for giggling in front of the FBI agent.

She let him wriggle free. "Why did you want me to wake up?"

"Agent Bell said you have something you need to tell me."

Her stomach lurched now. Jared was going to force her to tell their son right away? Before she'd even had coffee? She could smell the rich aroma of it; the scent had her mouth watering. Then she realized why the scent was so strong when Jared held out a mug to her.

He'd made coffee? He'd brought it to her?

He should be furious with her. He had every right. She'd only seen that brief flash of resentment. Where was his anger? She searched his face but could find no trace of it. His eyes weren't hard at all; they looked almost haunted.

Like he was afraid.

She was afraid, too. And not of a voice on the phone or a face in the window. She was afraid of the reaction her son might have when he learned the truth. She suspected Jared shared that fear.

"Alex wanted to know why I was sleeping on the couch," he said.

"You weren't sleeping," Alex said. "You were just lying there with your hand on your gun." Her precocious little boy missed nothing.

Jared had been protecting them. Her and his son.

She could see from the dark circles beneath his eyes that he hadn't slept at all. And he was so tense that a muscle twitched along his heavily shadowed jaw.

"I didn't know what I should tell him," Jared said. He wouldn't want to tell a child about a threat. "He didn't believe that's the way all FBI agents sleep."

Alex snorted. "They would be too tired to catch bad guys if they never closed their eyes."

He was definitely his father's son—too smart.

The corners of Jared's mouth turned up into a slight smile of amusement and pride. "He didn't buy that I had too much coffee, either…"

"He wasn't jumpy," Alex said, "like you get when you have too much coffee."

She nearly sputtered on the sip of coffee she'd just taken. Given that Jared had had his hand on his gun, she was glad that he hadn't been jumpy. He might have shot their son if Alex had exploded out of his bedroom like he usually did. "FBI agents can't be jumpy," she said.

Alex nodded as if she'd just made a good point. With his intelligence, she always wondered what he would become. A doctor. A lawyer. An FBI agent...

The possibilities were endless for him...as long as whoever was watching her caused him no harm. She was glad that Jared knew now that Alex was his son. She should have told him so much sooner.

And she could wait no longer to tell their son. "Jared stayed last night because we need to tell you something."

Jared sucked in a quick breath as if bracing himself for what she was going to reveal. But he already knew. He just didn't know how Alex would react.

Neither did she.

"What?" Alex asked. "Are bad guys after us? Is that why he stayed?"

"No," she assured her son. "Nobody's after us—" She hoped. *You're being watched*...

"But the man looking in my window—"

"Was just a reporter," Jared said.

"They were here about Aunt Lexi," Rebecca explained.

Her little boy nodded. He had seen Aunt Lexi's face on the news before—had overheard her story before Rebecca had been able to find the remote and shut off the nightmare.

But the remote couldn't shut it off. Only Jared catching the killer could stop the nightmare.

"Then what did you want to tell me?" he asked.

Panic had her pulse quickening, and she glanced at Jared. Should she tell? Did Jared even want to be a father?

That muscle twitched again in his cheek, but he nodded in response to the question she hadn't even had to ask him aloud. They'd once been that connected—that in sync that they'd spoken to each other's thoughts. And when they'd made love, they had instinctively known where to kiss, where to touch each other.

She shivered with another kind of awareness. But then Alex tugged on her arm, and his voice went all soft and shy as he fearfully murmured, "Mommy…"

She shrugged off her thoughts of Jared and focused on her child instead. Like his father, he also deserved the truth. "I want to tell you the answer," she said, "to that question you keep asking me."

His brow puckered with confusion. "I ask a lot of questions."

She almost smiled. He certainly did. All his teachers exclaimed over how inquisitive he was—that was how he had skipped first grade and was already in second. But she was too nervous to be amused as she clarified, "The one question I haven't answered yet."

He sucked in a quick breath. "Who's my daddy?" Then he glanced at Jared as the answer dawned on him. "Are you my daddy?"

Jared's throat moved as if he was swallowing hard. Choking on emotion? Then he gruffly replied, "Yes."

The little boy stared at him, his blue eyes narrowed in speculation. "We don't look alike."

"No," Jared agreed. "You look like your mother."

"And your aunt Lexi," Rebecca added. She clung to the fact that a part of her sister lived on in her son. It made Lexi's death seem less final to her.

But Alex was focused on Jared now. His voice quavered as he asked him, "Why haven't you ever come to see me before?"

Jared glanced at her, leaving the explanations for her to make. The explanation or the excuses. But there was no excuse for what she'd done.

She had to swallow hard, choking on guilt, before she answered, "Jared didn't know that you were his son—until last night, until after you were already in bed."

"You should have woke me up," Alex said. "You should have told me." He must not have wanted to miss another minute with the father she'd denied him for six years.

"I should have told you both a long time ago," Rebecca admitted. And she hoped that they could both forgive her someday.

"Why didn't you?" Alex asked.

She couldn't answer that honestly. It was too complicated for even a child as bright as Alex to understand. She wasn't sure she understood herself why she'd never told them. "I didn't know how…"

"To get ahold of me," Jared finished for her. "I've been really busy."

"Catching bad guys?" Alex asked him.

Jared nodded. "Trying to." As if on cue, his cell phone rang. He hesitated, letting it ring a few times before pulling it from his pocket.

He may have just found out he was a father, but he was also in the middle of a murder investigation. "I have to…"

But he clicked off the phone without answering it. Then he continued, "I have to leave."

"You got a bad guy to catch now?" Alex asked. Now the longing was in his gaze as he stared up at his father. He wanted to get to know him—wanted to be with him.

Jared nodded. "I'll be back, though," he said. And he crouched down to Alex's level. "I'll spend time with you, getting to know you."

Alex nodded but tears shimmered in his eyes.

Then he threw his arms around his father's neck and clung to him.

And Rebecca suspected there were tears in Jared's eyes, too, as his arms closed around Alex's small body. But she couldn't see clearly through her own tears.

Chapter Seven

Jared's head had finally stopped hurting. Now the pain was in his chest—his heart specifically. It ached with loss. With fear.

He shouldn't have left Becca and Alex. Not after the threat. And not after Alex had learned Jared was his father. Had he already let down his son?

"What's the 9-1-1?" he asked as he walked into the office of the chief of the Chicago Bureau of Federal Investigations. If anyone else had sent him the text, he would have ignored it. But if he ignored Chief Special Agent Lynch, he would have been taken off the case, at the least, and out of a job at the most.

Lynch stood over his desk instead of sitting in the chair behind it. He could have been impatiently waiting for Jared—since he'd had to drive to the police post and take a helicopter to Chicago. Or he could have been just standing because the man rarely sat. Despite his position, Lynch was no bureaucratic paper pusher.

"The Butcher has claimed another victim," the chief said. From the dark circles beneath his eyes, he didn't appear to have had much more sleep than Jared had. Like Jared becoming a profiler at a young age, Lynch had become a Bureau chief at a young age. But in the past six years, he'd aged—getting more lines on his face and gray in his hair. The serial killer eluding them had affected him, too. "That's a 9-1-1—one I thought you would have called yourself, Bell, after you identified those remains as Amy Wilcox's. Where have you been since you made the death notification?"

"Following up on a lead." But the photo of Lexi and Amy Wilcox wasn't why he had gone back to Becca's so late the night before.

The chief arched a dark brow over skeptically narrowed eyes. "Lexi Drummond's sister?"

"She's been threatened," he said.

"Why?" Lynch asked. "Is she engaged?"

"No." At least Jared didn't think she was. He hadn't asked her about a possible fiancé or even a boyfriend. He'd been too consumed first with his case and then with her revelation that he was a father. "But she received a strange call late yesterday afternoon—someone warning her that she's being watched and that she's in danger."

"So you put a protection detail on her?" Lynch asked.

"I don't want to take any chances," Jared said. And he wouldn't with Becca and his son. At least not with their safety. Dare he take a chance to try to act like a father to his son? Would it hurt the boy more if he tried and failed or if he didn't try at all?

Lynch uttered a weary-sounding sigh. "You're right. With the Butcher, we can't take any chances. We have to catch this bastard. *Now*."

"Nobody wants him caught more than I do, sir," he replied.

Lynch sighed again. "That's not true. Someone else wants him caught more—the victims' families. That's why I called you here. Amy Wilcox's fiancé is in the conference room. He has questions."

"When I made the notification, I promised I would keep them apprised of the investigation," he said, "that I would let them know when we discovered any new information. It hasn't been that long—I have no new information."

"He has questions," Lynch repeated. "Even if you don't have any answers yet, he needs to ask those questions. Go. Talk to him. Maybe ask some questions of your own…"

Jared had been keeping the chief apprised of his investigation, too, so he reminded him, "I already interviewed Troy Kotlarz as a possible suspect. He doesn't fit the profile." The profile he'd begun after the second victim was found and that he'd added to with each new victim. White male, thirties, single, charming but with few friends, professionally successful, personally unsuccessful—either jilted at the altar or broken engagement. Narcissist with a sadistic streak.

Lynch shrugged. "He may be worth another look."

The chief had become the chief because he'd earned the position by being a damn good agent. So Jared nodded in agreement. "I'll talk to him."

But he hesitated outside the conference room. The man had experienced a loss that Jared couldn't imagine. Becca wasn't even his fiancée but the thought of her just being in danger...

His heart pounded fast and furiously in his chest. She had protection. She and Alex would be safe. He had to believe that so that he could focus on his job. He opened the door and stepped inside. "Sorry to keep you waiting, Troy."

Kotlarz was a big man with prematurely thinning hair. His reactions and movements were slow. He seemed the exact opposite of the young and vivacious Amy Wilcox who'd been so athletic and adventurous. "I have no place else to be," Troy replied. "Your coroner hasn't released her body yet, so her parents can't plan her funeral."

Jared nodded. "We want to be thorough. We will catch him." And there he went—making that promise he had no business making.

Troy jerked his head up, his eyes wide as he met Jared's gaze. "You have new information?"

"Not yet," Jared admitted. "Or I would have called you. Why did you come down here?"

"I know you can't release her body yet," the other man replied. "But when can you release her things?"

"Things?" And why was it so easy for the man to talk of his fiancée's body? He was lucky to have a body to bury; Becca hadn't had one. Maybe the chief's instincts were still as sharp as ever.

"The engagement ring I gave her," Troy said. "That was my grandmother's. I really need to get that back."

Jared bit the inside of his lip and nodded. But he pulled out his phone and checked the list he'd made of everything recovered from the crime scene. "However, I don't see any record of a ring among her personal effects."

Troy gasped. "Do you think someone stole it from the scene?"

Why would he think first of a cop or a crime scene tech? Why wouldn't he blame the killer? Unless he was the killer? But if he was the killer, wouldn't he have taken the ring when he killed her?

And why would he have killed the other women?

That was why Jared had ruled out the man as a suspect. He had no motive for killing the others. There was no connection between him and any of the other women…except maybe Lexi Drummond.

"We'll search for the ring," he assured the other man. "Do you remember anyone ever calling Amy 'Root Beer'?"

Kotlarz shook his head. "No. She never even drank soda."

"Her initials…"

"Oh…" The man didn't just react and move slowly; he thought slowly.

Maybe it was Jared's pride that didn't want this man to be a viable suspect—since he couldn't conceive how Troy would have eluded him for six years.

"Did Amy ever mention going to a support group for women who suffered from domestic abuse?"

The man's face reddened and finally he moved quickly, jumping up from his chair. "I never hurt her!"

"She was in this group—" or so Becca thought "—six years ago."

"I met Amy six months ago."

And they were already engaged? That would have seemed odd to Jared if a couple other agents had recently married women they hadn't known long. Even Reyes was talking marriage.

"Did she ever talk about an abusive ex?"

Troy's eyes widened with sudden understanding. "You think he could have done this to her? There was some guy in high school who gave her a rough time. I don't remember his name. And her parents didn't know about him."

"I'll find out," Jared assured him.

"And you'll find the ring?" the man asked him hopefully.

He seemed to want the ring more than he wanted his fiancée's killer found. Jared offered him a vague nod before showing him out.

"What do you think?" Dalton Reyes asked as he followed Jared into his office.

Files, with a thin sheen of dust, covered his desk. Because of the prior case and his concussion, Jared hadn't spent much time in his office. And he didn't want to be here now, either. He wanted to be with Becca and Alex.

"I think Troy Kotlarz is a jerk," he replied, "but I don't know if he's a killer." He would find and interview Amy's high school boyfriend, though. He had another suspect to find, too— the one he'd promised Becca he would interview again. Lexi's former fiancé.

Reyes said, "Well, I've got good news."

"The crime lab found something? DNA?" Jared needed some evidence—any evidence—to lead him to the real killer. And convict him.

Reyes shook his head. "That must've been some concussion if you think they got results back in less than a day. This isn't a damn TV show, you know."

Jared sighed. "If only it could be that fast…"

Reyes sighed, too. "Unfortunately this is the real world. But the real world can be fast, too. Penny Payne called."

"Is she a witness?" Jared asked. For six years he'd been looking for a witness. "Someone from the bridal shop?"

"She owns a wedding chapel in River City, Michigan," Reyes said.

"River City?" No victim had been abducted from there, but he knew the place. "That's where Special Agent Nick Rus has been working a case—for a year now."

"Yeah, investigating the police and district attorney's office," Dalton replied. "The corruption runs deeper than he realized. Guess he reconnected with some family, too."

"Rus has family?" Jared was surprised. He'd known the other agent a long time. Hell, they even shared an apartment in Chicago—when either of them was actually home. Nick hadn't been for the past year. But when he'd been there, he'd never mentioned having any family. Jared had identified with that because he'd been an only child, too. Like Alex…

With no one else to play with, he'd focused on school and excelled. Would Alex? His son looked nothing like Jared—except for being small for his age. Did he have any other of his characteristics? Or, because they'd never been around each other, were they nothing alike?

"You sure you should have checked yourself out?" Dalton asked. "You just zoned out. Are you feeling all right? Should I take you back to the hospital?"

"I'm fine," Jared insisted. "Just wondering if you got hit in the head, too. I don't know why you're talking about some wedding chapel in River City."

"Nick recommended Elizabeth and I get married there. Penny Payne is the woman who runs it. Her family is all bodyguards, so she can provide protection, too. She handles everything. She called me because she had a cancellation. Elizabeth and I are getting married next weekend!"

"Next weekend?" It was crazy to consider a marriage now. "That's too soon." It didn't give him enough time to find the killer and prevent him from trying to kill Elizabeth. When she'd first been found, the media had dubbed her the one who'd gotten away from The Bride Butcher. The killer would no doubt want to prove that she wouldn't have gotten away from him.

"Feels like forever to me," Dalton said.

Jared snorted in derision. "You must've gotten hit in the head. I know you love Elizabeth, but you're putting her in danger."

"It'll be fine," Dalton insisted. "This killer isn't going to get past professional bodyguards and FBI agents. So are you in?"

Jared had to be in—he had to make sure nothing happened to Dalton's bride. "Of course."

"So you'll be my best man? I asked you last night, but you never answered me."

He'd been distracted the night before. "You were serious about me being your best man?"

He hadn't thought he was. Dalton Reyes had many friends—many more friends than Jared had made in the Bureau or outside of it. He was still the loner he'd grown up as—whereas Reyes had never met a stranger.

"I told you that Elizabeth and I feel like you helped bring us together. And you nearly died trying to protect her and little Lizzie."

"So this is a pity request?" Jared teased.

Reyes snorted. "What's your deal, Bell? Why is it so hard for you to accept that I actually want you to stand up with me?"

Had that been his problem with Becca? That he hadn't been able to believe that she could have actually cared about him? He hadn't just been an only child; he'd been an only child of parents who'd given him little time or attention.

His doctorate was in criminal psychology; while he was no criminal, he knew his childhood had affected him—had made it difficult for him to form or accept attachments. But he had a son now. He needed to change. And maybe this was a way to start. He was honored that Dalton would want him to stand up with him. They hadn't known each other long, but then they'd been through a lot recently. "Sure."

"Bring a date, too," Dalton advised.

"Date? What are you talking about?" He shouldn't even be thinking about attending a wedding—not with a murderer on the loose. But this killer had been on the loose a long time, and Jared had already given up too much in his pursuit of him. He'd given up Becca.

He'd thought he was acting in her best interests. That he needed to let her go so that she could move on—go back to med school, go back to her life. Instead, she had created a life—their son.

"I saw on the news that you went to visit Lexi Drummond's sister," Dalton said. "Bring *her*."

If her anonymous caller was to be believed, she was already being watched; she was already in danger. The last place he should bring her would be a wedding.

REBECCA HAD REFUSED to stay locked inside her house in protective custody. She wasn't even

certain she was in danger. For a threat, it had
been vague. So, with a sheriff's deputy following her, she had brought Alex to school and she'd
gone to work.

Maybe it wasn't just that she hadn't wanted to
be confined inside her house like a prisoner but
that she hadn't wanted to be in her house now
that Jared had been in it. She'd kept replaying
that morning—him and their son waking her
up with coffee.

And questions…

Maybe that was another reason she'd brought
Alex to school and gone on to work. She hadn't
wanted to keep answering his questions about
Jared—or not answering them. His questions
had made her realize how little she really knew
about a man she'd thought she'd loved.

Had Jared been right six years ago? Had she
only imagined herself in love with him so she
wouldn't have to deal with the terrible loss of
her sister?

Six years had passed now. She'd dealt with
that loss—because she'd had no choice and because Jared had given her a wonderful gift. Alex
had filled most of the hole that Lexi had left. But
nobody had filled the hole Jared had left. She'd
tried; she'd dated. But she'd felt about no other
man the way she'd felt about Jared.

That she still felt about him. She'd wanted his
kiss the night before. And this morning she'd

wanted him to crawl into the bed with her—like their son had. She wanted to be close to him—as close as they'd once been.

She expelled a shaky breath and grasped the handle of the exam room door. She had to focus on her job—had to focus on the people she could help since Jared refused to accept her help. Sure, he'd said he would interview Harris again. But she suspected he was only humoring her. He didn't believe that Lexi's fiancé had killed her, so why would he believe that the man had killed her friend?

"Good afternoon," she greeted her next patient as she stepped inside the room.

"Good afternoon, Ms. Drummond," the man greeted her before she'd even given him her name.

And the clinic was so informal that the badge on her coat had only her first name. She lifted her gaze from the laptop in her hands to the man perched on the exam table. And her breath shuddered out in revulsion.

She had seen this man just the day before—staring in her son's bedroom window. "What are you doing here?" she asked Kyle Smith.

According to the clinic laptop, he'd checked in at the desk with the complaint of stomach cramps. He wasn't doubled over or flinching, though. He looked perfectly healthy to her and perfectly evil, wearing a wide, self-satisfied grin.

"I didn't get the chance to talk to you yesterday," he said, "what with Special Agent Bell calling the local authorities to report us for trespassing."

Unfortunately, he hadn't spent the night in jail since he'd been on the news later that evening—at the scene where Amy Wilcox's body had been discovered.

"You were trespassing," she said. "And you're trespassing now."

He shook his head but not a blond hair moved on his head, as if lacquered down or as artificial as his orange-looking tan. "The clinic is open to the public."

"To patients," she said. "Not reporters. You need to leave."

"I came here for treatment," he said. "You can't turn me away. Haven't you taken an oath to do no harm?"

She wanted to harm the man for the scare he'd given her son and her. "I'm a physician's assistant," she said. "Not a doctor. I've taken no such oath." She opened the door and called out, "Security."

The clinic had none, but she suspected that the sheriff's deputy was still hovering around on Jared's orders.

Kyle Smith jumped down from the exam table, but instead of walking out, he came closer and shoved a mike in her face. "So FBI special agent

Jared Bell spent the night at your house," he said. "Are the two of you back together?"

She gasped at his audacity and his knowledge. He must have been the reporter who had discovered their relationship six years ago. The press had given Jared a real hard time about being unprofessional. She had wondered then if Jared had broken off their relationship to save face and his career. Her heart beating fast with fear, she backed away from Kyle Smith—into the hall. How had he known that Jared had spent last night at her house? Was he the one watching her? Was he the danger to her?

"Your son is his," the reporter continued. "Alex Drummond's birth certificate confirms it. You listed his father as Jared Bell." His snide grin widened. "Does Special Agent Bell know yet that he's a father?"

"A woman is dead," she reminded him. "Why does my personal life hold any interest for you?"

"You're the story," he said. "It started with your sister and you and Agent Bell."

The murders had started with Lexi. But Rebecca had nothing to do with them. "Leave me alone!"

Finally, the deputy rushed down the hall, his hand on his gun. "Ms. Drummond, are you okay?"

She shook her head. "No, please show Mr. Smith off the premises."

"I'll be back," he told her—again with that wide grin—as the deputy escorted him out.

She was still shaking as she headed toward the front desk. Hadn't the intake nurse recognized the reporter? Why had she let him back?

Before she could ask, Sylvia called out to her. "You have a call, Rebecca, on line three."

Jared. Maybe the deputy had already called him about the reporter. She stepped into a private office off the reception area and picked up the phone. "Hello?"

Her breath, still coming fast from her confrontation with the reporter, echoed in the phone. But no one spoke to her. "Hello?" she said again. Maybe Sylvia had told her the wrong line. She was reaching for another button when that raspy whisper spoke to her.

"Becca…"

She shivered. "What do you want?"

"For you to be careful," the voice ominously replied. "You're in danger."

Chapter Eight

After a sleepless night, Jared should have been exhausted—so exhausted that he should have been back at his apartment in Chicago, in his bed. But determination kept him going. He'd made promises. And this was one promise he wouldn't break. Unlike his promise to find a killer.

He'd promised his son he would return. And he stood outside Becca's house again, waiting for her to open the door. He'd already rung the bell twice. He was reaching for the button again when she finally opened the door. But she blocked the entrance—as much as she could with her slender frame.

She wore some kind of long T-shirt-looking dress that clung to every curve. And her hair was long and loose around her shoulders. The setting sun caught in the blond tresses, making them shine and shimmer.

His breath caught and his pulse quickened at

her beauty. And his attraction to her. He should be angry with her. He should be resentful. He had a right to know that she was pregnant with his baby—that she'd had his child. But she'd kept that secret for six years.

"You shouldn't be here," she told him, her voice terse with irritation and frustration.

She was angry with him? Was she mad that he'd left her and Alex that morning? He'd thought she understood that he was working a case—that he was trying to find Amy Wilcox's and her sister's killer. And all those other women…

"Why not?" he asked. Maybe she wanted him working the case instead of spending time with her.

Or maybe Alex didn't want to see him. Heat flushed Jared's face with embarrassment over the present he held under his arm. He'd been a fool to think that any toy could make up for the six years he'd missed of the little boy's life.

Her face reddened as she replied, "Kyle Smith knows you spent last night here. He showed up at the clinic today and wanted to interview me about it. Then I got that call after he left…"

The sheriff's deputy had already told him about the reporter showing up and about the call she'd received. It had already been traced back to a burner cell. He hadn't known, though, why Smith had showed up to harass her.

Jared cursed, then flinched as the little blond-haired boy squeezed between his mother and the doorjamb. "I—I shouldn't have said that," he told Alex. Some father he would make, teaching his son words no child should hear.

The little boy shrugged off the incident. "Mom swears sometimes, too."

Becca's face flushed a brighter shade of red. "Alex, I do not."

He jerked his head in a nod. "You do," he insisted. "Especially when you're driving."

"I—I…" she sputtered and then laughed. "Okay, maybe I do. Sometimes…"

"She does," Alex said. Then he reached out.

Jared thought he was reaching for the present and held it out. But the little boy grabbed his hand instead and tugged him over the threshold.

Becca still stood in the doorway, so Jared collided with her soft frame. His body pressed against hers. They were so close but not close enough. His skin heated and muscles tensed as desire overwhelmed him. Did she feel it, too?

He stared down into her beautiful face. Her bright blue eyes widened, and her breath escaped in a gasp. But then Alex tugged harder on his hand and pulled him through the door and into the living room.

Becca remained in the open doorway. Maybe looking for Kyle Smith…to see if he lurked outside as he must have the night before. How else had the man known Jared had spent the night?

And why hadn't Jared, during his vigil, noticed the reporter lurking around?

He needed to improve his protection duty skills—especially with Becca being in danger.

"Did you catch the bad guy?" Alex asked.

A pang of regret struck his heart—for so many reasons. He shook his head. "Not yet."

Alex's little hand squeezed his. "You will," the little boy assured him.

And another pang struck Jared's heart. How could his son have more confidence in him than Jared had in himself? Of course he'd vowed to others and to himself that he would catch the killer—even if it took the rest of his life. But he heartily hoped that it didn't take that long—that he would find him soon—before the man had the chance to abduct and murder another bride. So he vowed again, "I will."

Becca made a noise that drew his attention. He expected it to have been a snort of derision but she sniffled instead, as if fighting back tears.

Even though he didn't understand why she was so emotional, he wanted to comfort her. But when he had tried to comfort her six years ago, he hadn't been able to stop at just comfort. He'd taken advantage of her vulnerability and given in to that overwhelming desire he had for her. While he hadn't given her real comfort, he'd given her a child.

An amazing child…

"I told my friends at school that my daddy is an FBI agent," Alex said.

"You did?" Becca asked the question.

Jared was too stunned to speak. His son had been bragging about him? He didn't even know him. Becca had obviously never talked about him to their son.

Alex nodded, but his mouth pulled down into a little frown. "But they didn't believe me. They think I made it up—that I made you up."

Jared squeezed the little boy's hand and offered assurance now. "I'm real."

Alex shook his head. "They said that I don't have a dad 'cause I never talked about him before and 'cause he's never been around."

And that ache returned to Jared's heart—that hollow feeling he'd had all day since he'd had to leave his son and stay away from him. From them.

Becca sniffled again before speaking in a voice heavy with guilt and emotion. "That wasn't your fault. That wasn't your father's fault, either."

"I told them that," Alex said. "I told them he was busy catching bad guys."

Becca released a breath that sounded like relief. Her son wasn't blaming her. But then she turned to Jared, and her gaze searched his face. Over the years he'd gotten good at hiding his emotions. So she might not see his resentment, but it was there—simmering inside him.

He wasn't as forgiving as the little boy. She should have let him know when she'd found out she was pregnant. She should have let him be a part of his son's life. He wasn't sure she was going to let him be a part of it even now that he knew Alex was his.

They hadn't discussed that. They hadn't discussed anything. And maybe she'd only said that about Kyle Smith knowing he'd spent the night in order to get rid of him before they could have the discussion they needed to have.

The little boy shrugged off his friends' reactions to his news and turned his attention to the brightly wrapped package Jared was holding. "Who did you bring the present for?" he asked. "Me or Mommy?"

"You, of course," Becca answered for him.

She expected no presents from Jared. After he'd failed to find her sister's killer or even her body, she probably expected nothing from him—especially after how he'd rejected her feelings for him.

"It is for you," Jared said as he handed the box over to the boy.

"But it's not my birthday," Alex said.

Jared had no idea when his son's birthday was. How far along had Becca been when he'd told her it was better that they have no further contact? After the way he'd treated her, he had no right to his resentment.

"And Christmas is a couple months away," Alex said.

"I owe you some presents," Jared said—for all those birthdays and Christmases he'd missed. "Go ahead and open it."

Instead of tearing off the paper, as Jared suspected most kids his age would have, Alex studied the package. He narrowed his eyes and tilted his head as if he could see inside the box. Then he weighed it in his hands. "I don't think you brought me a gun…"

"Alex!" Becca exclaimed with a gasp. Then she glanced at Jared as if worried that he actually might have bought the child a gun.

He knew very little about kids, but he knew better than to arm one. "It's not a gun," he told them both.

"A car?" Alex asked.

He should have bought him a toy car. Didn't all little boys love cars? He hadn't been all that interested in cars at that age, though. Of course he'd always been a little odd. So he had no idea if he'd bought his son something he would like.

"Just open it," Becca encouraged the boy.

Alex sighed but settled onto the floor with the present. Then he proceeded to remove each piece of tape—slowly and methodically.

"He does this with every present at Christmas," Becca said. "It takes two days for him to finally open them all."

And the resentment fired back up, making Jared remark, "I wouldn't know."

But he should have known. He should have been there every Christmas, watching his son take days to open all his presents. He should have been there for birthdays and T-ball games. Did Alex play T-ball? Or soccer? Or was he as unathletic as his father had been?

"I'm sorry," she murmured, her voice low and soft and close to his ear since she'd leaned toward him.

He felt her breath and her warmth and inhaled her sweet, summery scent. She smelled like flowers and sunshine. And her closeness heated him.

Jared leaned toward her—tempted to kiss her and not to comfort her. Or to punish her. He wanted to kiss her, simply because he wanted her.

But Alex uttered a soft gasp.

Jared turned his attention to his son. The little boy stared down at the box he'd finally unwrapped. He should have brought him a car. What had he been thinking?

"I can take it back," he offered. "And get you something else, something you'd like…"

"Like?" Alex looked up at him and blinked his long lashes quickly as if fighting back tears.

Oh, God, he'd really screwed up.

Then Alex stood up and launched himself at

Jared, wrapping his arms around his waist to squeeze him tight. "I love it!"

And Jared's heart shifted in his chest as emotion—as love—overwhelmed him. A day ago he hadn't known the child existed; now he couldn't imagine a world without him in it. He patted the little boy's back and head. "I'm so glad."

And not just that he'd bought the right thing. But he was so glad he had a son. He'd never thought about being a father before. But now that he was one...

He was glad.

"What is it?" Becca asked curiously.

Alex pulled back from Jared's embrace. His voice shaking with excitement, he replied, "A lie detector test! Want to try it out, Mommy?"

Her mouth fell open in such surprise that Jared laughed.

"Or do you want to go first, Daddy?"

And his mouth fell open in shock and delight. But before he could answer his son, his phone rang—work dragging him away once again from a special moment. Now, instead of resenting Becca, he resented the career he'd once loved so much.

"Mommy will have to go first," he told Alex. "I have to take this."

Hopefully it would be good news—that the lab had finished processing the evidence from the crime scene. Hopefully it wouldn't be news that another woman had been abducted...

REBECCA STARED AFTER Jared as he stepped outside. Her first thought was that his call was work related. Then another thought quickly chased that from her mind. What if it was personal? What if Jared had a girlfriend? Or fiancée? Or wife?

She'd never asked him. But if he'd been wearing a ring, she would have noticed. Not that all married men wore rings nowadays.

And it would be naive of her to think that he hadn't dated in the past six years. Even she'd gone on dates—hoping to find someone with whom she could share the life she'd built for her and Alex.

But none of those men had held her interest— because none of those men had been Jared. He was Alex's father; he was the man who should be part of the boy's life.

She'd been selfish to keep them apart. It had broken her heart to learn that Alex's friends hadn't believed he really had a father. She blinked hard, fighting back tears of regret and guilt.

"Mommy, can I hook you up to the lie detector?"

She was afraid of what he might ask her, so she stalled. "You have to take it out of the box

first. And you should have Ja—your father—
help you with that."

"He's probably gotta go chase a bad guy,"
Alex said. But instead of being resentful that
his father might have to leave again so soon, he
beamed with pride.

"He'll come back inside and let us know." If
it was work calling him, she could find out another way. She picked up the remote and turned
on the TV.

And Kyle Smith, with his glib grin, appeared
on the screen. If something had broken in the
case, or the killer had abducted another girl, this
reporter would know about it. So, albeit reluctantly, she turned up the volume. If whatever
Smith was saying was too graphic for little ears,
she would click the mute button.

The door creaked open as Jared stepped back
inside, but she barely registered his return. Her
attention was riveted on what Kyle Smith considered a news report.

"I have confirmation—" the man held up
a birth certificate "—that Lexi Drummond's
nephew is FBI profiler special agent Jared Bell's
son. Agent Bell spent last night at the home of
Rebecca Drummond and his son, Alex. Maybe
if the profiler had focused more on his job than
the first victim's sister, he would have caught the
killer before now."

Her hand shaking as fury and embarrassment

overwhelmed her, Rebecca struggled with the remote trying to shut it off. Jared's hand covered hers and his finger pushed hers down onto the button that mercifully shut off the *news* report. "I'm sorry," she murmured. "I didn't think just anyone could pull a birth certificate."

But she hadn't been able to bring herself to list her son's father as *unknown*. Because she'd known. Jared should have known, too.

She lowered her voice to a whisper. "I shouldn't have presumed to put your name down—"

He squeezed her hand. "I'm glad that you did. I would have been more upset if my name wasn't on it."

His hand was warm and strong, wrapped around hers. Her skin heated and tingled from his touch. It had been like that when they'd made love—his touch made her tingle. Made her hot...

Even after all these years, she still wanted him. And she found herself leaning closer.

Then Alex laughed.

She jerked back and turned toward her son. "What's so funny?"

"They're going to feel stupid tomorrow that they didn't believe me."

Jared chuckled.

Rebecca was not amused about her life being made so public. She glanced at the windows, wondering if Smith or other reporters lurked out there. A shadow passed in front of the glass. "You need to leave," she told Jared.

He shook his head. "After that I think it's more important I stay."

"You don't have to chase a bad guy?" Alex asked.

"Not tonight," Jared said. "My call was from another agent—letting me know about this *news* report." A muscle twitched along his jaw.

"Are you sure you shouldn't go chase bad guys tonight?" Rebecca asked with a meaningful stare, so that Jared would get the hint. She wanted him to leave.

But Jared was looking at the window, too, and reaching beneath his jacket.

She gasped. "Someone is out there?" She turned toward Alex. It wasn't just her life made so public; his had been, too. And that put her son in whatever danger she was in.

Somebody is watching you…

She shivered. "Alex, you need to go to your room."

He glanced up from his new toy. "Why—"

"Go." Jared said just the one word. He didn't shout it or say it with any particular emphasis. But Alex jumped up and rushed down the hall.

"You, too," he told Rebecca as he withdrew his gun.

But she didn't obey him like their son had. "This is my house…"

Jared ignored her as he moved quickly toward the door and jerked it open.

A scream caught in her throat as fear overwhelmed her. Jared hadn't had to chase down the bad guy. He had found them. Her sister's killer stood at her door.

Chapter Nine

"What the hell are you doing here?" Jared asked as he tightened his grip on his weapon.

Six years ago he'd thought Becca was wrong about this man. Jared hadn't believed Harris Mowery had murdered her sister. But he still hadn't liked the guy.

"You contacted me, Agent Bell," Mowery replied. He wore the same smug grin that Kyle Smith always wore. Both men were narcissists—concerned only with themselves and incapable of empathy. Both of these men fit the profile for the Bride Butcher. "You want to talk to me."

"At the Bureau office," Jared said. "Or I would have come to you." If he could have tracked down the man.

"Instead, I came to you." Harris's dark grin widened. He was all white teeth and shiny bald head. Even six years ago, his head had been shaved; he'd probably done it the moment his hair had begun to thin. He was the kind of man who would not tolerate imperfection—in himself or in others.

"How did you find me?" Jared asked. But he was more concerned that he'd found Becca and Alex.

"You're news, Agent Bell." He peered around Jared to where Becca was probably standing.

She should have left the room like their son had. Jared blocked the doorway with his body, refusing to let the uninvited guest past him.

"You're both news, Rebecca," her almost-brother-in-law addressed her. "Congratulations."

She said nothing in return. She was probably either too angry or too scared to speak. She fully believed this man was a killer. Jared was definitely more suspicious of him than he'd previously been—especially after he'd worked up a more complete profile of the killer.

"That news report just ran," Jared pointed out. "You wouldn't have been able to get here so quickly unless…" Unless he'd been close. Unless he was the one watching Becca, as she'd been warned. But why would he have alerted her to his presence?

Just to toy with her? To scare her more?

"Kyle Smith called me," Harris admitted, "gave me a little advance report."

"You answered his call," Jared remarked. "You two must be close."

Harris sneered. "I'm not a fan of reporters. But Mr. Smith has proven to be most informative."

Jared had already been angry with Kyle Smith for invading Becca's privacy. Now he was furious and a curse slipped through his lips.

Harris chuckled. "He's not a fan of yours, either. He suggested I sue you for slander."

"I've never named you as a suspect," Jared said.

Harris tilted his head, and despite the grin on his face, his dark eyes were hard with resentment. "But you've questioned me and made the media aware that you have."

"Lexi was your fiancée."

Harris nodded. "Yes, she was."

But just like six years ago, the man wasn't exactly mourning her loss. Not like Becca had mourned her and continued to mourn her.

Jared blamed himself for that—because he hadn't given her closure.

"Have you reopened Alexandra's case again?" Harris asked.

"Lexi," Becca corrected him. Her voice was low but hard with hatred.

He ignored her, his focus on Jared now. "Is that why you left me a message that we needed to speak again?"

"I've never closed Lexi's case," Jared said.

Harris shrugged. "But you can't have any new

leads in a case that old. You don't even have a body." He snorted disdainfully.

And Jared's fury built. He'd always understood why Becca hated this glib guy. He'd abused her sister. And instead of being upset or concerned when she'd gone missing, he'd been angry.

That anger was why Jared hadn't suspected him, though. If the man had killed her himself— or even hired someone to do it—he wouldn't have been furious that she was gone. He would have been happy.

Like he seemed now.

"I actually called to find out where you were the day Amy Wilcox went missing." He gave the exact date and time that Amy had been taken, kicking and screaming, from that bridal boutique dressing room.

And Harris's grin widened. "I was with Priscilla Stehouwer. We spent that weekend at a bed-and-breakfast in the country. I can give you her number." He glanced down at the gun Jared still held. "If you have a free hand…"

Jared was reluctant to reholster his gun. He couldn't risk Becca's and Alex's safety. Not if she was right about this man. "You can leave it on my voice mail," he said. "I already left you my number to call me back."

"Did you buy this alibi, too?" Becca asked him.

Now the man spared her a glance—one so

hard and hateful that Jared tightened his grasp on his weapon. "Of course not. Priscilla is my fiancée," he said.

Then maybe this alibi wouldn't be as ironclad as his had been for Lexi's disappearance. Jared definitely intended to question Priscilla Stehouwer. And maybe he would let it slip about those pictures they'd found in Lexi's journal.

"But I shouldn't need an alibi," Harris said. "I didn't even know Amy Wilcox."

"Lexi says differently," Becca said.

Harris looked at her again—with pity and disgust—as if he thought she was claiming to have had an actual conversation with her sister. "Alexandra is dead."

Her body had never been found, but Harris seemed awfully damn certain of that. Because he knew where her body was buried? Or just because he'd heard all the reports—that she couldn't have survived that much blood loss?

"She wrote it in her journal," Becca explained. "She said that you met Amy Wilcox and you didn't like her."

Harris shrugged. "She wrote a lot of stuff in that journal that wasn't true."

And if Jared told the fiancée about those photos, Harris would undoubtedly take Kyle Smith's advice and sue him for slander.

"It was the truth," Becca said. "But I wouldn't expect you to admit that—"

"Becca," Jared cautioned her. He didn't want her getting sued, either. Or worse...

He didn't like Harris Mowery showing up at her door. He didn't like it at all. "You need to leave," he told the man, and he stepped forward to usher him out.

But Mowery didn't step back. "So will you two be getting married now?"

Becca gasped, and Jared pushed, forcing the man backward. But still Harris persisted, "Since you have a son together, you should."

Jared shoved him completely out the door.

But Harris yelled out, "And soon!"

Jared followed him out and pulled the door shut behind himself, so that Mowery couldn't talk to Becca anymore. "What the hell are you up to?" he demanded to know.

Harris shrugged. "I don't know what you mean, Agent Bell. Can't I just want Alexandra's sister to be happy?"

"If that were true, you wouldn't have showed up at her house, knowing the way she feels about you." Jared narrowed his eyes in a hard stare. "It's you, isn't it?"

Harris finally stepped back voluntarily from the front door and the illuminating glow of the porch light. He walked down the driveway toward his car and the darkness. "You already ruled me out as a suspect, Agent Bell," he reminded him. "You said so yourself."

Jared followed him and clarified. "That was in Lexi's murder." And maybe he'd done that too quickly. He intended to recheck that first alibi and definitely the one for Amy Wilcox's murder.

"One serial killer murdered all those women," Harris said. "That's something else you've always stated—at least according to Kyle Smith."

Damn Kyle Smith. That was someone else Jared intended to interrogate. Why the hell had the reporter given this man Becca and Alex's address?

"You're the one," Jared repeated and then continued, "who's been threatening Becca."

"Someone's been threatening Rebecca?" Harris sounded surprised, or maybe he was just a better actor than Jared had realized. "Why would someone do that? Unless…"

Jared waited—as the man wanted him to—in the dark as night began to fall.

Harris clicked the lock on his rental car and opened the driver's door, spilling light onto the driveway. "Maybe you two are already engaged…?"

Jared shook his head. "I haven't seen Becca in years."

"She never told you she had your son?" Harris shook his head. "Maybe she's more like her sister than I realized. Alexandra had her secrets, too."

"Yes, she did," Jared agreed. She should have told her family that Harris was abusing her. "Remember to text me your fiancée's phone number." He didn't give a damn if the guy sued; he was going to warn the woman.

And the minute Harris drove away, Jared called back the protection duty he'd released when he'd arrived. He needed protection on Becca and Alex 24/7—even when he was around them. And still he worried that it might not be enough to keep them safe.

HER HANDS SHAKING, Rebecca pulled the blankets over her sleeping son. He'd fallen asleep in his bed even though there'd been a killer in their house. He obviously felt so safe that he slept peacefully.

Rebecca would never feel safe again. She shivered and considered crawling into bed with her son—to hold him. But he didn't need comfort. She needed comfort.

And a gun. The front door creaked open again, unsettling her. But instead of hiding in her son's room, she hurried down the hall to the living room. Jared stood inside. Alone.

"Is he gone?" she asked.

"Yes."

"But you can't guarantee that he won't come back," she said. She couldn't stay here. "Alex and I will have to leave."

"I called back the protection detail," he said. "You'll be safe."

She would feel safer if he stayed, too. But she'd already told him he couldn't spend the night. "Alex fell asleep," she told him.

He glanced down at the game their son had left on the floor. "He seemed so excited about his present."

"He was. He is," she assured him. "But he's had a lot of excitement today. It must have exhausted him." She glanced down at the gift Jared had chosen for their son. "Is that really a toy?"

"I didn't steal it from the Bureau," he said, his lips curving into a slight smile.

"Too bad," she said. "If it was real, we could have hooked Harris up to it." Just saying the man's name brought back all her fear and anger and frustration. And as the emotions overwhelmed her, tears stung her eyes, and she began to tremble.

Instead of offering her the comfort he once had, Jared walked back toward the door. He was leaving?

Of course she'd told him he couldn't stay, but that had been before her sister's killer had paid her a visit—taunting her to get engaged. So he could kill her like he had Lexi, like he had all those other women.

Instead of opening the door, Jared turned the dead bolt. "The protection detail is out there," he said. "But I'm still not leaving."

She uttered a sigh—of relief. Then she was

in his arms. She wasn't sure which one of them had moved—him or her. But she clung to him.

One of his hands was on her back, holding her to him. The other was in her hair. He tipped her head back, and then his mouth covered hers. This was no tentative kiss. But even their first kiss hadn't been tentative. It had been like this one—explosive: making her heart beat fast and erratically. Making her head light and her body heat and tingle.

Nobody had ever kissed her like Jared did—passionately, thoroughly. And nobody had ever made her feel like Jared did—passionate and desperate.

Desperate for his kisses. Desperate for his love. But she'd never had his love. And now she didn't even have his kisses as he pulled back.

"I'm sorry," he said between pants for breath. "I—I didn't mean to do that…"

She was glad that he had. She'd been longing for his kiss since he'd first showed up at her house.

"I only meant to hold you," he said, "to comfort you. But every time I touch you, I lose control."

"That comforts me," she said. To know she wasn't the only one feeling that overwhelming attraction and desire. Especially now. After knowing what she'd kept from him—their son—he should have been disgusted with her.

Instead, his fingers stroked along her cheek, and he stared deeply into her eyes. "You are so beautiful…"

Lexi had been the beautiful one. The vivacious one. Rebecca had been the smart one. The hardworking one. But Jared made her feel beautiful; he had always made her feel beautiful—even when grief had ravaged her. He'd helped her find the beauty in life. Then he'd given her the most beautiful gift of all: Alex.

"You should hate me," she said, "for keeping our son a secret from you."

"I should," he agreed, but his fingers continued to stroke along her cheek. Then his thumb moved across her lower lip—back and forth. "But I can't."

"I'm sorry," she murmured.

"Me, too." Then he replaced his thumb with his lips and kissed her again.

And again—until her knees weakened. Before her legs could buckle beneath her, he swung her up in his arms and carried her down the hall to her bedroom. He laid her on her bed and stood over her, passion glinting in his eyes. "Do you still want me to leave?"

She shook her head. Then she reached out for him—for the buckle of his belt and unclasped it. His hands covered hers, stopping her before she could reach for the zipper of his pants. "Are you sure?" he asked.

His erection pressed against the zipper. He wanted her. Even though he should be furious with her, he wanted her. And Rebecca had never stopped wanting him. Six years. It had been too long.

"Very sure," she replied.

And then he joined her in the bed, his hard body pressing hers into the mattress. His mouth covered hers, kissing her deeply.

She wanted more than kisses, though. She tugged his shirt free of his loosened pants. Then she reached for the buttons running down his chest and abdomen. As she undid each one, she revealed an inch of skin and muscle. When his shirt was open, she pressed kisses to his chest.

He groaned. And she smiled, pleased that she affected him as much as he affected her. But her kisses must have snapped his control because he moved quickly then, removing clothes from both their bodies until they were naked—their skin flushed with desire.

He pushed her back against the pillows, and he kissed her everywhere. Her neck, her shoulder, her elbow…and each fingertip.

She sighed with pleasure. But then he kissed other places. Her breasts, her abdomen and lower…

Her breath caught as pressure wound tightly inside her. She wanted more. Needed more.

And he gave her more. She pressed her hand over her mouth, muffling a cry as pleasure overwhelmed her. Then she reached for him, wanting to please him with her mouth. He groaned again as if he were in pain. And he rolled, pinning her playfully beneath him. He teased her some more—with his lips and his fingers.

She squirmed and shifted against the mattress. "Jared, please…"

"I am going to please you," he promised.

She arched and rubbed her hips against his. And tangled her legs with his. Then she kissed his shoulder and the bulging muscle in his arm. And his chest again.

"Becca…"

She didn't correct him. She would rather be Becca than Rebecca.

Then he parted her legs and joined their bodies. She was ready for him, but still she had to shift, had to arch, to take him deeper. But he moved, too, pulling out before thrusting deep again.

She bit her lip to hold in a cry of pleasure. It felt so perfect. So right. She clung to him, meeting his thrusts, moving with him until the pressure that had built inside her, that unbearable pressure, burst. She pressed her lips against his shoulder to hold in a scream of ecstasy.

Then he tensed before his body shuddered, as

he joined her in release. His skin damp against hers, he clutched her closely in his arms. "That was…"

As wonderful as it had always been between them. But she waited for him to call it something else. A mistake. That was what he'd thought the last time they'd become lovers, that he'd made a mistake.

But he said nothing more. He just held her tightly, so tightly that she felt safe enough to fall asleep. But she wasn't surprised when, hours later, she awoke alone. Her sheets tangled, but empty.

Then she heard the rumble of a deep voice. He wasn't gone. He hadn't deserted and rejected her as he had six years ago. At least not yet…

Then she heard the high-pitched squeal of Alex's laughter. And she knew why Jared had stayed. For their son.

She dressed quickly and joined them in the living room. Father tickled son as they sat on the carpet, the lie detector hooked to the little boy. It looked like a blood pressure cuff hooked to an Etch A Sketch with a bunch of squiggled lines on it.

"You are lying," Jared said. "You're definitely ticklish."

"Did the test say I'm lying?" Alex asked between giggles.

"I don't think he needed the test to determine that," Rebecca said. "You're definitely ticklish."

"Mommy's up," Alex said. "It's her turn now."

Even if the test was just a toy, she didn't want to be hooked up to it. But she couldn't tell her son no. So she let him strap the cuff to her arm.

"So, Mommy," Alex said, "do you ever swear?"

She groaned. "Yes…"

He giggled again. "Are you the tooth fairy?"

"Alex!"

"Santa Claus?"

She reached out and began to tickle him. He squirmed and protested. "No, you have to answer the questions yes or no."

"No, no," she said and hoped the machine wasn't real.

Alex squinted at the screen and shrugged. "I don't know. Daddy, you ask her a question."

She sucked in a breath—afraid of what he might ask her. Afraid of even looking at him. But he moved closer, so that he could see the screen her son studied. And she breathed in the scent of him—some intoxicating combination of soap and coffee and musk. He must have used her shower and made coffee again. She looked up and lost herself in his amber-eyed gaze.

"What do you want to ask her, Daddy?"

He stared at her a moment, as if considering.

And she saw that he had many questions. But she never guessed what he would ask her. "Will you go to a wedding with me?"

Chapter Ten

Why had he asked Becca to Dalton Reyes's wedding? And why, in the days since he'd asked, hadn't he rescinded the invitation? It was too dangerous. But then even staying in her own home was too dangerous—with Kyle Smith broadcasting her address to suspects. So he'd convinced her and Alex to stay with him—at his condo in Chicago—instead of in their home. Surprisingly, Becca had readily agreed. But then he doubted she would ever feel safe in her house again now that Harris Mowery knew where she lived.

"Why?" he asked the reporter.

"Isn't that what I should be asking you?" Kyle replied as he settled onto a chair across the conference table from Jared. "Why did you ask me to come to the Bureau office? You finally realized you will need my help solving your case, Special Agent Bell?"

Jared patted the folder that lay on the table

between them. "It seems you wanted to be an FBI agent yourself."

Kyle's snide grin slid away, and he stared at the folder as if wanting to grab for it. "You had me investigated?"

Jared plastered on his own smug grin and replied, "It only seemed fair since you've been investigating me."

"Ouch," Kyle said and pressed a hand to his chest as if Jared had stabbed him. "So instead of focusing on finding the serial killer who's eluded you for six years, you've wasted time going after the reporter who revealed your dirty little secret."

Alex was not a dirty little secret. He was an amazing kid. A wonderful gift. Jared curled the hand on the folder into a fist that he wanted to swing hard into the reporter's face.

Smith's superior grin had returned. "Sounds like I have my next exposé…"

"And instead of covering the real story—about the murders—you're creating a story about me," Jared said. "Is that because you're jealous that I have the job you really wanted?"

Kyle snorted. "I'm sure I make more money than you do, Agent Bell. And I'm definitely better known."

"Seems like your career really didn't take off until you covered Lexi Drummond's disappearance."

"Murder," Kyle corrected him with the same certainty as when Harris Mowery had said it.

Sure, there had been too much blood found for her to have survived her wounds. But that information hadn't been released to the media—until Kyle had reported it. At the time Jared had thought that the reporter must have bought the information off someone in the crime lab or maybe even within the Bureau.

Now he considered that there was another way that Kyle Smith could have known Lexi was dead—because he'd murdered her. As a profiler, Jared knew that killers liked to make themselves part of the investigation—by helping search for the victims or providing false witness. No one had made himself more a part of the investigation than Kyle Smith.

Like men who failed to make the fire department became arsonists, maybe men that failed to make the Bureau became serial killers. Trying to prove themselves better than the men they hadn't been able to become…

"You're awfully certain Lexi Drummond is dead."

Kyle snorted. "So are you—even though you failed to find a body. No wonder Rebecca Drummond never told you she had your son." The man laughed. "And it wasn't like you would ever figure it out for yourself…"

Jared could have pointed out all the killers

he'd caught over his career. So many, many killers who were behind bars or dead because of him. But Kyle Smith wanted him to be defensive, so then he'd know that his barbs had struck their target. Jared wouldn't give the petty man that satisfaction.

"You're a great investigator," he falsely flattered the man. Anybody could order a copy of a birth certificate nowadays—thanks to the internet. "So why haven't you found Lexi's body?"

Kyle tensed. "What do you mean?"

"You've been working this case as long as I have," Jared pointed out. "But you don't seem to care about the victims..." Only one other person didn't care—the killer. The Butcher was a sociopath with no capacity for empathy for the victim or the families he devastated when he took away their loved ones. And he was beginning to think Kyle Smith was a sociopath, too. Was he the killer? He certainly fit most of the profile Jared had formed.

"You don't even seem to care about the killer," Jared remarked. "But then I guess that you really don't want him caught."

Kyle's Adam's apple bobbed as he swallowed convulsively. "Why would you say that?"

Jared shrugged. "A couple of reasons..." One was that he was the killer. "*He* made your career. Without him—"

"I would still have a career," Kyle said as he jumped up from the table.

Jared tilted his head, then shook it. "I'm not so sure about that…"

When he caught the killer, Kyle Smith might be behind bars. He grinned at the thought of slamming the cell door shut on the slimy reporter.

"I'm leaving," Kyle announced but he hesitated, as if not sure he was really free to go.

"I'm not done with you yet," Jared said. "I have many more questions for you. I want to know if you knew any of the victims and if you had an alibi for each of the abductions."

Kyle dropped heavily back onto the chair. "You're treating me like a suspect?"

"Yes."

"Why? Is this because I told the world you took advantage of a victim's grieving sister?" the reporter fired the questions at him. "Is this your form of revenge?"

Jared gave him a pitying grin. "You really wouldn't have made it as an agent."

"You—"

Jared held up a hand to stop the insults. "If you've taken any criminal psychology courses, you would know that the perp often makes himself part of the investigation."

"I've just been doing my job," Kyle protested.

"Giving Rebecca Drummond's address to Harris Mowery? That was part of your job?"

The man's face flushed an even darker shade than his artificial tan. "I didn't do that."

Jared didn't believe him.

"He probably found it the same way I did—checking property tax records."

Maybe he could have—maybe he'd already been watching her, like the caller had warned Rebecca.

"So that's what this is about," Kyle mused. "Because you think I gave out her address to the man she swears killed her sister."

"Why would you do something like that?" Jared asked. "Why would you report about *her* life—about *my* life?"

Kyle offered that snide grin again. "It's not personal, Agent Bell."

But it felt very personal. Was there some reason that Kyle didn't like him or Becca? Or was his animosity only because Jared had the job Kyle had wanted? The man was petty. But was he that petty?

Or was he a killer?

Jared slid a legal pad and a pen across the table. "Start recounting your whereabouts during the time of every abduction," he ordered. "And tell me if you have any personal connection to any of the victims."

Then he patted the folder he'd already compiled. "And then we'll see if your answers match mine."

Kyle picked up the pen with a shaking hand. Either he was nervous because he had something to hide, or he was angry over becoming a suspect. Resentment hardened his eyes. The man was going to hate Jared more than he already did.

So he would probably retaliate again. What form would that retaliation take? More public humiliation for him and Becca? Or something even more personal?

BECCA HAD TAKEN Alex out of school and had taken a leave from work. Hell, what she'd really taken was a leave of her senses.

Moving in with Jared in Chicago? That was more frightening than Harris Mowery knowing where she lived—because she was afraid she was falling for Jared again. Or maybe she'd never stopped...

But at least he would keep their son safe. Jared had even enrolled Alex in a new school—the one where he'd gone, for gifted children. Alex loved it; he was actually challenged. Becca wasn't sure, even if Harris was finally arrested, that she would go back to Wisconsin.

Maybe she needed to look for a job in the city—like she'd always wanted. But first, she had to find a dress for the wedding to which Jared had invited her.

"This is my wife's favorite store," Agent Blaine Campbell said as he held open the door to a little dress boutique squeezed in between a bank and bakery.

"You really didn't need to come with me," Rebecca said. "I could have found it on my own." And she felt a little awkward shopping with the burly blond lawman. She'd never even gone shopping with Jared.

"Jared doesn't want you going anywhere alone," Blaine told her. Needlessly.

She was already aware that Jared didn't want her having a minute alone—in case someone might threaten her again.

"He's wasting Bureau resources protecting me," she said. When those resources would be better used trying to find Amy Wilcox's killer.

"You've been threatened," Blaine said. "And he's not really using Bureau resources. I'm not on the clock right now."

"Then why…?"

"I'm a friend of Jared's."

"Like Dalton Reyes?" That was whose wedding Jared had invited her to.

Blaine chuckled. "Not that close. I'm new to the Bureau, but I got to know Jared when he was helping protect the bride-to-be for Dalton."

"That's who he got hurt protecting?"

Blaine nodded. "Probably why Dalton asked Jared to be his best man."

"Jared is best man at this wedding?"

Blaine chuckled again. "Yes, he is."

That put more pressure on her finding a nice dress. Her wardrobe consisted of only casual clothes, business casual and play clothes. Nothing suitable for a wedding at all. That was why she'd had to go shopping. But now she would be attending this wedding on the arm of the best man.

So she focused on the racks of dresses, trying to find the perfect dress—the dress that would make Jared proud to call her his date.

But she was more than a date. She was the mother of his child. And the woman who'd been sharing his bed since he'd shared hers the night that Harris Mowery had showed up at her door.

What were they doing? What the hell was she doing—risking her heart on a man who'd already broken it once?

"I'm actually surprised Jared agreed to be his best man," Blaine continued, "since he thinks the wedding is such a bad idea."

"He does?" she asked. "Doesn't he like the bride?"

"He likes Elizabeth," Blaine said. "We all do. She's an incredibly strong woman. But Jared's worried that the Butcher is going to go after her."

Rebecca shuddered. "Isn't her fiancé worried, too?"

"Dalton is too impatient to wait to make Elizabeth his bride," he said. "And he's found a very safe place for them to get married. With all the bodyguards and FBI agents in attendance, it'll be safe. Jared must have changed his mind about it, too."

"Because he agreed to be best man?"

"Because he invited you."

Jared wanted to keep her safe. She knew that, but why? Just because it was his job? Because she was the mother of his son? Or because he had feelings for her, too?

She pulled a blue dress from the rack and a peach-colored one. But the peach would wash out her complexion, so she moved to put it back.

"Wait," Blaine said. "That would look good on Maggie."

Rebecca smiled over the man's obvious love for his wife. Then her smile slid away as a pang of jealousy struck her heart. She wished Jared felt that way about her.

"You should take a picture of it and send it to her," Rebecca suggested. "And I'll try this one on." She glanced at her watch. Alex's school wouldn't be done for a while. She'd rather be working than shopping. She would definitely need to check with the local hospitals for any openings for a physician's assistant. But in the meantime, she grabbed a couple more dresses from the rack to try on; shopping would kill some time today.

Blaine followed her to the dressing room. But one of the retail clerks hurried over to stop him. "Sir, you can't go into the dressing rooms!"

The woman was in her fifties with frosted hair and a frosted glare. She studied Blaine's hand and then glanced at Rebecca's bare one. Rebecca's face heated with embarrassment over what the disapproving clerk obviously thought. Blaine wore a wedding ring, and she didn't.

He flashed his badge. "I need to check out the dressing room and make sure no one's back there."

"There is no one back there," the woman haughtily told him.

"I need to check it out myself," he insisted and added beneath his breath, "or Jared will kill me.

"I'll look and leave," he promised her.

She sniffed with disdain but allowed him to look. "It's safe," he told Rebecca.

"Of course it is," the woman said. She took the dresses from Rebecca and led her back to one of the rooms. "Do you need any help?"

"No," Rebecca replied. What she really needed was to be alone. If Jared wasn't with her, someone else was—watching and protecting her. She needed a moment to breathe without anyone worrying about her safety.

So she took her time trying on the dresses. The ones she'd grabbed at the last minute weren't flattering. The A-frame waistline of the first made her look like she was expecting again. She tensed for a moment. But then shook her head. She couldn't be. And if she was, she wouldn't be showing yet.

She unzipped that one and shimmied into another. It was a pale cream. Too close to white to wear to a wedding. She was reaching for the zipper when she heard something.

Hadn't Blaine assured her that the dressing rooms were empty? Had he let someone else into them? Maybe the judgmental clerk had insisted on checking on her.

She drew in a breath, bracing herself for no longer being alone. She'd only wanted a few minutes to herself. But then the lights blinked off, plunging the dressing room into total darkness. With no windows in the back of the store, the blackness was all-enveloping.

Was this how Lexi had been grabbed from the bridal boutique? Had someone shut off the lights and attacked her in the dark?

She parted her lips to utter a scream for Blaine, but a hand clamped over her mouth. And a familiar low and raspy voice whispered in her ear, "Look how easily I got to you."

Oh, God. This wasn't just another of those eerie warnings. This was it—her abduction. But she wouldn't go anywhere without one hell of a fight. So she kicked her legs and swung her fists as she fought for her life. For her son who needed his mother.

For Jared...

She couldn't leave them like Lexi had left her. Forever.

Chapter Eleven

The interview with Kyle Smith had been an exercise in frustration and probably futility. The man hadn't been able to readily supply alibis—which probably meant he had no reason for any. Most people didn't remember exactly where they were and who they were with a week ago, let alone years before. Kyle had remembered only his alibi for Amy Wilcox's abduction. But he hadn't remembered any for the others. He hadn't even remembered the other victims' names but for Lexi.

Natalie Gilsen, Madison Kincaid, Heather Foster, Tasha Taylor and Eden LeValley had been forgotten as far as Kyle Smith was concerned. Jared hadn't forgotten them—hadn't forgotten how he'd failed them. If he'd caught Lexi's killer—like he'd promised Becca—all those other women would have lived. They would have married their grooms and probably been raising kids by now.

But just because Kyle Smith hadn't remembered the other women's names didn't mean he hadn't killed them. Jared passed the folder over to another agent. "I've started compiling information on Kyle Smith. I need you to delve more thoroughly into his past and any connection he might have to the victims. Also check to see if he was ever jilted—left at the altar or broken engagement."

The younger agent widened her eyes. "You think *Kyle Smith* could be the Butcher?"

Jared nearly laughed. The young woman obviously had a crush on the obnoxious reporter. "It wouldn't break my heart if he was."

"Oh," she said with a nod. "I saw that report he did about you."

"But Agent Bell would never be unprofessional enough to use the Bureau for revenge," a deep voice said.

Jared turned toward his boss. Despite it being several years since he'd done any fieldwork, Chief Special Agent Lynch still moved with surprising silence. He'd easily snuck up behind Jared in the hall. But maybe he wouldn't have snuck up so easily if Jared hadn't been so tired. His nights weren't sleepless because of protection duty, though, but because Becca shared his bed. Fortunately, his apartment was in a high-security building. Harris Mowery or whoever the Butcher really was wouldn't get to her and Alex there.

But Jared didn't want her with him just for her and Alex's protection. He wanted Becca in every way…

With only a meaningful glance, Chief Lynch sent the young agent running for her desk. That was why he was in charge. Jared braced himself. Not that the chief hadn't already reprimanded him for crossing the line with a victim's family member. He'd even threatened to take him off the case. That was why Jared had had to take the call outside Becca's house the night his boss had phoned—the same night Harris Mowery had showed up at her door.

The same night Jared had spent crossing the line again—in Becca's bed.

"I'm not," Jared said, "using the Bureau for revenge."

Lynch nodded and agreed. "Smith is a viable suspect. A national network didn't pick him up until he covered Lexi Drummond's murder."

So he'd used Becca's sister's murder to further his career. "I'm going to try to find a link between them." Or between Smith and Harris Mowery. Why had he given the man Becca's address? He'd claimed he hadn't, but Jared had learned to believe nothing a suspect said.

His cell phone vibrated in his pocket. "Excuse me, sir…" He needed to at least check and see who was calling. He pulled out the phone. After recognizing the number on the caller ID, he fumbled to answer it. "It's Alex's school. Hello, this is Jared Bell."

"Mr. Bell, this is Julie VanManen from Saint Agnes School for Gifted Children."

Why was the principal calling? He couldn't imagine Alex getting into trouble. Maybe out of boredom in a regular classroom. But he loved his new school. "Is everything okay, Ms. Van-Manen?"

"I hope so," she replied. "No one has arrived to pick up your son yet."

Jared's blood chilled. Becca had never been late to pick up Alex during the week in which they'd been staying with him. "I—I'll come right away."

Alex was probably nervous that no one had picked him up. And Jared was scared to death that no one had. His hand shaking, he punched in the number for Blaine Campbell. Even though Special Agent Campbell worked the bank robbery division, his true specialty was protecting women. He had that white knight gene—the one that made him the protector of every damsel in distress.

Not that Jared had considered Becca a damsel in distress. He'd had to insist on the protection detail. She'd thought he was overreacting—until Harris Mowery had showed up at her door.

Blaine's phone went directly to voice mail. He tried Becca's even though he suspected she had shut it off to avoid any more ominous calls. It went straight to voice mail, too. Jared cursed.

"I'll pick up your son," Chief Lynch offered. "You find Agent Campbell."

Jared hesitated a moment.

"I will protect your son," Lynch vowed.

Jared wasn't worried about him protecting Alex. He was worried about him scaring the crap out of him. The guy was intimidating to special agents who'd faced down death and endured torture.

Lynch chuckled, and suddenly he looked twenty years younger. "I am a father, too, you know."

Jared had had no idea.

"I know how to handle kids."

Jared nodded acceptance as he started walking toward the elevator. "I'll call the school and let them know you have my permission to get Alex." He pounded the down button for the elevators, impatient for the car to arrive. If he wasn't on the tenth floor, he would have taken the stairs. Maybe he still should...

But he could hear the car coming, rattling in the shaft as it rose. He punched in Blaine's phone number again. Where the hell was he? Where the hell was Becca?

His guts tightened with dread and fear. She couldn't be like those other women—she couldn't be missing. Why would the killer have abducted her? She wasn't engaged.

But he'd thought about it—had thought about how nice it was having Becca and Alex living with him. He'd thought about how amazing it was sleeping next to her, his arms wrapped tightly around her warm, soft body.

Had just thinking it endangered her?

"ARE YOU SURE you're okay?" Blaine asked, his voice deep with concern and guilt.

Rebecca shook her head and winced as pain radiated throughout her skull.

"I should have taken you to the hospital," Blaine said. He had brought her back to Jared's apartment instead. He led her over to one of the leather couches in the living room.

She was still shaking from the close call she'd had, so she dropped onto the closest couch. The leather shifted beneath her. Alex always giggled when the leather creaked and squeaked beneath him.

"Alex!" she said. "We forgot to pick up Alex!"

Blaine's face paled. But she didn't know if it was because he'd forgotten the boy, too. Or if it was because the apartment door rattled as someone turned the knob.

Blaine drew his weapon and pointed the barrel toward the door. "Who's there?"

"It's me," Jared said as he thrust open the door and hurried inside the apartment.

"Did you pick up Alex?" The school would have called him when she hadn't showed. Wouldn't they? He'd given his name and his cell phone number.

"The chief is picking him up," Jared replied as he dropped onto his knees in front of her. "Are you okay?"

"Are you?" Blaine asked. "You just said the chief is playing nanny."

Rebecca's stomach lurched. Alex was usually shy around strangers, especially men. And from Blaine's tone, she discerned the chief wasn't exactly warm and fuzzy. "We should go get him."

"Chief Lynch will bring Alex here," Jared said. "Why didn't you two pick him up? What happened?" He turned toward Blaine and glared at his friend. "Why didn't you pick up your damn phone?"

Blaine patted his pocket. "I may have dropped my phone back at the boutique."

"What the hell happened?" Jared asked again. He turned back to her. "And what the hell were you doing at a boutique?"

"I needed a dress for Dalton Reyes's wedding," Rebecca explained. "It was a dress boutique." She knew what he was thinking—what he was worrying about. "Not a bridal boutique."

But still, someone had attacked her in the

dressing room. Or had she attacked him? She touched the back of her head and winced again.

"You're hurt," he said. And his fingers replaced hers, rubbing over the bump beneath her hair.

Despite her fear and shock, she reacted to his touch—to his fingers in her hair. And his closeness…

He was so close that she could feel his breath on her face. She could see the muscle twitch in his cheek from his tightly clenched jaw. He was so handsome.

Would this attraction ever lessen? Would her skin ever stop tingling when he touched her?

"It's just a bump," she assured him.

"You could have a concussion," he said.

She shook her head. "I never blacked out." Although she had seen stars for a moment. "And I'm not nauseous. It's not a concussion."

"I tried to take her to the hospital," Blaine said. "But she refused."

"Because I know it's not a concussion." She'd treated enough head injuries in the ER that she would have recognized had it been a concussion.

Jared turned toward his friend again and studied him through narrowed eyes. "You were supposed to protect her. How did she get hurt?"

Blaine shook his head. "I don't know how it happened. I checked the dressing room before I let her go back. There was nobody back there."

Jared cursed, but then he turned back to her. "Somebody tried grabbing you in the dressing room?"

"Somebody grabbed me," Rebecca replied.

Jared's neck swiveled toward Blaine again. "How? Where were you?"

"He couldn't go into the dressing room with me," she said. "And he checked it before I went inside."

"Nobody was back there," Blaine reiterated.

"So what happened?"

"I heard something," she said. "I thought it was just the clerk coming back. Then the lights went out." Her voice cracked as, in her mind, she returned to the dressing room and that moment of sheer terror when she'd thought the Butcher was going to abduct her. "And someone grabbed me, pressing a hand over my mouth so I couldn't scream."

She hadn't been able to call out for help.

"The power had gone off in the whole store," Blaine said. "But just in the store. There were lights on across the street."

"So you knew something was up and got to her in time?"

Blaine regretfully shook his head. "No, she fought off the attacker herself. I never even got a look at him. That's why I better get back down to the store. I'll get the security footage from all the cameras in the area." He patted his empty pocket. "I also have to find my phone."

The minute the door closed behind Agent Campbell, Jared focused on Rebecca again. His hand gently cupped her face. Were his hands shaking slightly? Was he that upset?

"Are you really all right?" he asked. And he stared intently into her eyes—as if he could see what she had seen—what she had endured.

She wasn't all right. She was shaking—scared and mad. But she nodded and lied. "I'm fine."

"Did you see anything?" Jared asked. "Anything that might help us identify him?"

"It was too dark," she said. "So dark that I couldn't see anything at all." And that was the reason for most of her frustration. She had been so close…but she had learned nothing.

"Did you notice anything else at all?" he asked. "A smell? His height? His build?"

She furrowed her brow as she realized something. "I don't think he was that tall. I head-butted him to get away. That's how I got the bump on the back of my head."

"And if he was that much taller than you, you wouldn't have hit his head," Jared said.

But then she shrugged. "I don't know, though. He was leaning down and whispering…"

"Did you recognize his voice?" he asked.

"I think it was the person who's been calling me," she said. That must have been why the voice had seemed familiar.

"It didn't sound like anyone else you've heard?" Jared persisted.

He obviously had a suspect in mind. For the Butcher...

She shook her head then, flinched as the throbbing intensified to pain.

"We can't risk your safety again," Jared said. "We're going to have to move you to a safe house—somewhere nobody can get to you— until the killer is caught."

"No," she protested as panic pressed on her lungs, stealing away her breath. She'd already given up her home—her job, her routine. "I can't be locked up for six years."

Jared flinched now.

"I'm sorry," she said. He already blamed himself for all the murders since Lexi's; she shouldn't have added to his guilt. "I'm sorry. I know you're only trying to protect me."

She just wished she knew why. Because he was a lawman? Because of Alex? Or because he loved her?

"You're in danger," he said.

"That's what he said," she shared. "When he grabbed me, he said, 'Look how easily I got to you.'"

Jared cursed.

"Then he said, 'You're in danger. You have

to be more careful.'" And then she realized why she'd gotten away from him so easily. "It's not him…"

Jared uttered a ragged sigh of relief. "You wouldn't have gotten away if it was him," he agreed. "It wasn't the Butcher."

"Then who is it?" she wondered. "Who keeps calling me and warning me to be careful?"

Jared tensed again. "I hope it's not him. But it has to be. And he let you get away because he's just toying with you—scaring you for his entertainment."

Like Harris Mowery showing up at her house. She was right about him; she had to be right about him killing Lexi.

"Then why did he let me go?" She wasn't that strong. She wouldn't have broken away from him if he'd really intended to abduct her.

"Because you're not getting married…"

Apparently, Jared hadn't been tempted to ask her. He hadn't loved her six years ago. And he didn't love her now. Maybe that was a good thing—because until the killer was caught, she would never be able to get engaged. Because the minute she had a ring on her finger, she would be dead.

Chapter Twelve

Jared's hands shook as he straightened his bow tie, and sweat beaded on his upper lip. He couldn't breathe—in the windowless groom's dressing room. And worse yet, he couldn't see. He couldn't see outside the room to make sure that Becca and Alex were safe.

He wasn't the only nervous man in the groom's dressing room. Dalton Reyes's usual cocky nonchalance was gone. His hands shaking, he fumbled with his bow tie and cursed.

"Should've got a damn clip-on," he grumbled.

Jared smacked his hands away and tied the bow. "And that's why you picked me for best man."

"Actually, I had no idea if you knew how to tie a bow tie," Dalton said.

"So why'd you pick him?" Nicholas Rus asked as he joined them in the groom's room. "I didn't even know you two knew each other."

"He got his brains scrambled protecting my

fiancée—" Dalton's voice cracked with emotion "—my bride—and her daughter. So I figured I owed him."

Jared snorted in amusement. That was why he hadn't been able to say no to Reyes. He'd never had a friend like him. Usually, his friends were as serious and no-nonsense as he was—like Nicholas Rus.

While Reyes made Jared feel like he'd finally gotten invited to eat at the cool kids' table, he appreciated Nicholas's seriousness. Especially now.

"Are you sure this chapel is safe?" Jared asked him.

Nick grinned. "Absolutely safe. All of the guests are FBI agents."

Not all of the guests. Becca was out there—along with Alex. Fortunately, Alex had insisted on sitting with his new best friend—Chief Lynch. While Lynch hadn't been in the field for a while, Jared had no doubt the man could still handle himself—and an inquisitive little boy.

"And bodyguards are protecting the perimeter," Rus added.

Jared and Reyes shared a glance; apparently they'd both noticed the same thing about those guards.

"How come they all look like you?" Reyes asked. "Did River City have you cloned?"

A muscle twitched along Rus's jaw. "I reconnected with some family."

"I didn't know you had siblings," Jared said. And they'd lived together for a few years in Chicago.

"Neither did I," Rus replied.

Knuckles rapped against the door of the groom's dressing room. "Is Reyes ready?" a deep voice called through the door. Special Agent Ash Stryker probably should have been Reyes's best man because Reyes had been his. "Or did he go out the window?"

"There is no window," Jared called back.

"As I understand it, a groom has disappeared from this room before," Rus said.

"I'm here." Dalton chuckled and opened the door to Ash. "I was more nervous at your wedding. I have no doubts about marrying my bride."

He was nervous, though. Moments later, Jared, standing next to him at the front of the church, noticed the tension in the other man. He stood stiffly, barely breathing, until a vision in white appeared at the back of the church. Then he released the breath he'd been holding.

And Jared released the breath he hadn't realized he'd been holding, too. He'd been so worried that the Butcher would try for Elizabeth—just to prove that she wouldn't have been able to get away from him.

But the fitting for her wedding dress—at this very chapel—had passed without incident. Maybe the bodyguards and agents had proved too daunting for the Butcher. He hadn't dared try for Elizabeth because the risk of getting caught had been too great. Or he was focused on another target...

Becca.

Despite all the guests, Jared easily found her in the church. She, Alex and the chief sat a few rows back on the groom's side of the aisle. Sunlight shone through the stained-glass windows, making her blond hair shimmer like crystals. Even after being attacked in the dressing room at the boutique, she had bought a dress for the wedding.

She'd wanted to attend. But he never should have asked her. He should have locked her away in some safe house just as he'd threatened. But she was right; she couldn't hide until he caught the killer.

He had no new leads. No evidence tied Kyle Smith or Harris Mowery to any of the murders. That didn't mean that it didn't exist, just that he hadn't found it yet. He needed to find it. He needed to put this killer away.

Or he could never ask Becca to be his bride. He imagined her standing in front of him—a vision in white—her hands in his as they said their vows. But until the Butcher was caught, marrying her was just a daydream.

If he even asked her to marry him, she would definitely be attacked, and the killer wouldn't let her get away from him again. The Butcher would make certain she died before she could ever marry him.

REBECCA HAD NEVER felt so safe—with all the federal agents and bodyguards in and around the Little White Wedding Chapel. She'd also never felt as envious. As she waited in the receiving line in the foyer, she watched the bride and groom. While they hugged or shook hands with guests, they leaned against each other—constantly touching, always aware of each other. And so in love that it radiated from them like the sun shining through the stained-glass windows.

She probably looked at Jared the way the bride was looking at her groom; her gaze full of adoration. From the moment Jared had stepped out of the groom's dressing room, looking so damn handsome and debonair in that black tuxedo, Becca had been staring at him with love and attraction and adulation. But she doubted Jared had ever looked at her the way Dalton Reyes looked at his bride. His mouth curved into a wide grin, he stared at her as if unable to look away.

She was beautiful—with her vibrant red hair and creamy skin. She lifted the flower girl, who wore a lacy white dress, into her arms. With curly dark hair, the little girl looked nothing like her mother. But she was definitely hers—even though, as Jared had shared, Elizabeth hadn't given birth to the child. And Dalton looked at the little girl with as much love as he looked at her mother. They were a very happy family.

The family Rebecca wished she could give Alex. While she studied the bride and groom, she felt someone studying her. She shivered with apprehension as that warning ran through her mind again. *Someone is watching you...*

But when she glanced around, the person whose gaze she found on her was Jared. He peered around the guest shaking his hand, as if unable to take his gaze off her. She doubted it was because he loved her—like Dalton Reyes loved his bride. She suspected it was just because he wanted to keep her safe.

But still her skin tingled and heated from just the touch of his gaze. Would she ever not react to him? To his closeness? To his handsomeness? To his intelligence?

The line moved forward, probably because Alex had grown impatient with standing still and pushed ahead. His hand on Chief Lynch's, he dragged the older man along with him. The poor chief was filling the grandfather void Rebecca's father had left in the little boy's life.

Alex was as much a reminder of Lexi as Rebecca—maybe more—so her parents wanted nothing to do with him. That was their loss more than his, though. Alex had eased that unbearable ache she'd had after losing Lexi.

Jared hadn't ever talked much about his parents. Would they like being grandparents? Would they love the little boy? Had Jared even told them yet that he had a son?

She moved forward in the line, too, close enough that she heard what the man standing by Jared asked him. But that man and the chief were such tall, broad men that Jared wouldn't be able to see her anymore. There was no one else behind them; they were the end of the line. "So are you next?"

"Next?" Jared asked.

"First it was Blaine, then me, now Reyes," the dark-haired man said. She'd met him earlier; he was another FBI special agent—Ash Stryker. "So you're next, right?"

Reyes took his attention from his bride for a moment to smack Jared's shoulder. "Ash is right. And it seems like whoever's stood up as best man at the last wedding becomes the next groom. So you're definitely next."

Jared shook his head. "No way."

And pain stabbed Rebecca's heart at how adamant he sounded. She'd already suspected he didn't return her feelings, but she'd thought he cared about her at least a little. How else had he forgiven her for keeping his son from him? Or hadn't he forgiven her?

"Was Kyle Smith wrong?" Agent Stryker asked. "Isn't that little boy yours?"

Maybe Jared didn't believe Alex was his son. He'd never had a DNA test to prove it. He only had her word for it and his name on the little boy's birth certificate.

"He's mine," Jared said with a glance toward where Alex hung from the chief's arm.

"I figured you for an old-fashioned guy," Agent Stryker said. "After I saw that broadcast, I thought you would beat Reyes to the altar."

"Not a chance," Reyes said. "Nobody was going to beat me to the altar." He leaned back toward his bride and dropped a kiss on the top of her head.

She smiled up at him, her gray eyes shining with love.

And Rebecca's envy returned.

Stryker grinned at the newly married couple. Then he turned back to Jared. "Well, you can still get married next."

Jared shook his head again. "No. I can't."

She sucked in a breath that burned in her lungs. He had no intention of ever marrying her. While they'd been sharing his bed since she and Alex had moved in with him, it was all he intended to share with her. Not his heart...

But then he continued, "I can't put her in that kind of danger."

"You think marriage to you would be that rough?" Reyes teased.

"I think the Butcher wouldn't care how many

FBI agents and bodyguards were around," Jared said. "He would go after Becca for certain. He already has, and we're not even engaged."

The chief, thankfully, covered her little boy's ears, as the two of them moved along the line until they now stood in front of Jared. "I didn't think you believed the incident at the boutique was the work of the Butcher."

Rebecca didn't believe it. She wasn't engaged. But maybe that news broadcast had made the Butcher think that she soon would be. When he'd showed up at her house, Harris Mowery had been taunting Jared about proposing to her. He wanted her engaged, so that he could go after her—like he'd gone after Lexi and all those other poor women.

"We couldn't find anything on all the security footage Blaine turned up from the stores in the area," Jared said. "The guy that went after Becca was good at staying off camera—just like the Butcher always has."

Unless the Butcher was Kyle Smith. Jared had told her that he'd questioned the reporter. She considered it a waste of time. She knew who the Butcher was. She'd even begun to believe that Jared now suspected the same.

But he hadn't been able to break that damn alibi for Lexi's disappearance. And the man had provided another for Amy Wilcox's abduction. Maybe he would never be caught; maybe he would just keep killing more and more innocent young women.

"But you think he would risk getting caught—even with federal agents and bodyguards around—in order to grab Ms. Drummond?" the chief asked.

Jared's handsome face grim, he nodded. "He wouldn't be able to resist. It all started with Lexi Drummond. She was the most important to him."

"So her sister would be important, too?"

Jared nodded again. "So important that he's already messing with her—with the phone threats, with the confrontation in the dressing room."

"Then that's how you catch him," the chief matter-of-factly stated.

"What?" Jared asked just as Rebecca silently uttered the word herself.

"You propose to Ms. Drummond."

"To catch a killer?" Jared asked. "You want me to use her as bait?"

Of course he wouldn't propose because he actually wanted to marry her. He didn't love her—not like Dalton Reyes loved his bride. So much so that he hadn't been able to wait to marry her. No, Jared didn't love her—not like Rebecca loved him, like she had always loved him.

"But it might be the only way," Chief Lynch suggested softly, as his hands dropped away from the wriggling little boy's ears.

"What might be the only way?" the ever-inquisitive Alex asked. He stared up at all the adults, who probably seemed way too serious to him. He also had to wonder why the chief had covered his ears.

She was glad that he had; the little boy didn't need to hear that the Butcher might have already gone after his mother. And he certainly hadn't needed to hear anything about his parents getting married. He would get the completely wrong idea. He would think that they were in love, and all of them would become one happy family.

Rebecca knew better. Jared didn't love her.

She moved forward, so that she stood beside the chief again. "They're talking about catching the bad guy," she explained to her son.

The ultimate bad guy—the man who'd killed her sister. The man who would keep killing if he wasn't stopped.

And she was the key to stopping him. Even the chief thought so.

"I'll do it," she said. "I'll help catch the bad guy."

Alex's eyes widened in shock. "But Mommy, you're not an FBI agent."

No. She wasn't an FBI agent. She was a mother who had no business putting herself in danger. She knew that, and from the disapproval on Jared's face, he was thinking the same thing she was.

If it was any other killer, she wouldn't have risked it—probably not even if she knew she could save the lives of other women. But this was Lexi's killer.

She had to do this—for Lexi. She hadn't been around when her sister had needed her. Putting herself in danger wouldn't bring Lexi back, but at least Rebecca would be able to get her what Lexi had been denied until now. Justice.

"I'm just going to help," she explained to Alex. "The FBI agents will catch him." Hopefully before he could kill her as he had all the others.

Chapter Thirteen

Jared held his temper until Alex was out of earshot. The woman who ran the wedding chapel, Penny Payne, had taken him downstairs to where the reception was being held. She'd promised him cake. Like him, his son had a sweet tooth.

But even cake couldn't tempt Jared now, as anger churned inside him—unsettling his stomach.

After the auburn-haired woman disappeared down the steps with his son, he turned to his boss and Becca. "Absolutely not," he told them. "This will not happen. You are not putting yourself in danger."

She lifted her chin, her jaw tense, and her blue eyes hard with determination. "That's not your decision to make."

"It's not yours, either," he informed her. He turned to his boss. "You can't seriously be considering using a civilian to bait a serial killer?"

"Ordinarily, I would never allow it," Chief

Lynch admitted. Then he uttered a heavy sigh. "But we haven't been able to catch this man any other way."

"We won't this way, either," Jared said. Instead, he risked losing Becca—forever.

"You said yourself that he won't be able to resist trying for me," Becca said.

Jared bit off a curse. He hadn't realized she'd been listening when he'd said that. There had been so many people standing in the foyer then. Now it was only him, the chief and her. Everyone else had gone downstairs to the reception. He had to get to the reception soon, too. He had a toast to make—had a head table to sit at; he should have ignored Reyes's suggestion that he bring a date. He never should have invited Becca.

"And because you're not a trained agent, you're not equipped to deal with him," Jared pointed out.

"I got away at the boutique."

"You admitted he let you get away," he reminded her. "If he'd really wanted to abduct you, he would have. And he will if you pose as my fiancée."

She flinched. And he wasn't sure why. Because he'd told her that she wouldn't get away again? Or because he'd told her she would only be posing as his fiancée?

Did she want to be his real fiancée? Did she want to make their living situation permanent?

He wanted to, but not now—not like this—when it could put her in so much danger.

"I won't be part of this," Jared continued. She was already in too much danger for his peace of mind. He couldn't use her as bait and risk losing her forever. "I will not pretend to be your fiancé."

Her face reddened—either with temper or embarrassment. And she turned to the chief. "So assign another agent to act as my fiancé," she implored him. "There has to be someone else…"

"They're all married," Jared told her. "And as easily as Kyle Smith found Alex's birth certificate, he would find their marriage licenses."

She laughed. "Every FBI agent can't be married." She gestured toward one of the men walking around. "What about Agent Rus?"

The man she'd pointed at was actually one of the bodyguards that Reyes had joked was Rus's clone. But she must have met Nicholas earlier.

"He's on assignment here—in River City," Jared said. "And the killer will know it's a trap if your groom is anyone but me. He would have seen the story Kyle Smith did on us." Unless the killer was Kyle Smith, then he had run the story himself.

She expelled a heavy sigh of resignation and said, "So it has to be you."

He shook his head. "No, I won't put you in any more danger than you already are."

He wouldn't be able to live with himself if something happened to her. She meant too much to him—more than he was willing to admit to her. He was struggling with admitting it even to himself.

"You'll ignore a direct order?" Chief Lynch asked.

Feeling as if his boss had sucker punched him, Jared drew in a quick breath. "Is this a direct order?"

Instead of answering him, the chief turned toward Becca. "Will you give us a minute, Ms. Drummond?"

She nodded. "Of course."

Jared's stomach churned with anxiety now as she walked across the foyer toward the stairwell leading down to the reception area. He hoped one of his friends was available to protect her. But it was Agent Rus who met her on the stairwell and turned around to walk back down with her. While Nick was a friend, he wasn't Jared's first choice for her fake fiancé. But he probably only felt that way out of jealousy, because Nick had been Becca's first choice.

When had he become the jealous sort? He'd never been possessive of anyone before. But he'd never cared about any other woman the way he cared about Becca. She was beautiful and smart and a loving sister and a wonderful mother and a phenomenal lover. He couldn't lose her.

"She's safe," Chief Lynch assured him.

"She won't be if you use her as bait to lure out the Butcher." Because the Butcher wouldn't stop at scaring her; he would take her, and like Lexi, Jared would never be able to find her again. "You can't do this."

"We have to catch this killer," Lynch said with all his intimidating intensity.

"I know that," Jared said. "And I'm working on it."

"For six years," Lynch said.

"I have a profile."

"White male in his thirties—single," the chief paraphrased the profile. "Charming and affable on the surface but with a sadistic streak. You have a profile but no suspects that fit it."

"Harris Mowery abused his fiancée before she disappeared," Jared said. He certainly fit the profile.

"And he has an ironclad alibi for her disappearance."

Jared silently cursed that alibi. If only he could have disproved it. But he had another suspect. "Kyle Smith."

"Is charming and affable on the surface," Lynch agreed. "But sadistic?"

Jared nodded. "He's been relentless with Becca."

"And you." The chief's dark eyes narrowed. "But with her, too. Not the other victims' families—only Ms. Drummond. She is definitely the key to catching this killer."

"The bait," Jared corrected him.

"She volunteered," Lynch pointed out.

"She isn't equipped to deal with this killer."

"Agent Campbell said she handled herself well in the dressing room at the boutique," Lynch said. "You're not giving her enough credit."

"She's smart and strong," Jared said. "But the Butcher's other victims were smart and strong, too. I don't want her to become his next victim."

"I want her to become his last," Lynch said.

Panic gripped Jared's heart. "You're willing to sacrifice Becca to catch this killer?" That might have made sense in times of war or even in Ash Stryker's antiterrorism division. But Jared had never been a marine like so many of the other agents. He couldn't sacrifice any life for any reason. And he absolutely could not sacrifice Becca's.

"She'll be safe," Lynch said. "We'll protect her—just like we have Reyes's bride. And she'll be even safer when the killer is caught."

Jared couldn't argue with that. The best way to keep Becca safe was to catch the killer and put him behind bars for the rest of his life.

"I'll talk to Mrs. Payne about having another wedding here—yours and Ms. Drummond's." Then the chief walked away as if Jared had given his agreement to this crazy plan.

But he hadn't given Jared a choice; neither had Becca. She'd willingly put herself in danger.

He knew why—for Lexi. But from what he'd learned about Lexi, from Becca and from reading the young woman's own journals, she wouldn't want her sister risking her life. Not for any reason…

BECCA PROBABLY WOULDN'T have made it down the stairs without Agent Rus's hand on her arm to steady her. The minute she'd walked away from Jared and the chief, she'd realized what she'd just done, and she'd started shaking with fear. What the hell had she been thinking?

Like Jared had said, she was not a trained agent. She was a civilian. A mother.

Alex ran up to her the minute she stepped into the reception hall. The room was big and bedazzled with twinkle lights and flowers and streamers. "It's pretty, isn't it, Mommy?" he asked as he clasped her hand. He gazed shyly up at Agent Rus.

"Prettier than my room," Agent Rus agreed. "I understand you've been sleeping in my bed."

Alex smiled. "It's pretty comfy. Do you want it back?"

Rus shook his head. "No. I moved all my other stuff out. I think I'll be staying here."

So Jared had spoken the truth about Agent Rus's assignment in River City. He couldn't pose as her fiancé. But like Jared had said, after Kyle Smith's report, only he could. Would he? Or would he refuse even if the chief ordered him?

"Nice meeting you both," Rus said as he stepped away.

Alex's smile widened. "Did you hear that, Mommy?"

"What?"

"We can stay with Daddy forever," he said. "Agent Rus's room can be mine now."

Her stomach pitched with regret. Moving in with Jared had been a horrible idea—because it had given her son the wrong idea. And if he heard about their *fake* engagement, he would get entirely the wrong idea.

"We can stay in Chicago," she said. She'd already decided to make the move—for his new school. Not for Jared. She knew now that Jared would never marry her—not for real. And probably not for fake, either. So she hadn't put herself in more danger than she already was—at least not for her heart, only for her life.

She leaned down and swiped a dab of white frosting from the end of Alex's little nose. "I see you checked out the cake already."

"It's so big, Mommy!" he exclaimed with excitement—his wish to live permanently with his father momentarily forgotten. "And Mrs. Payne says it's vanilla and chocolate. I can have some after the bride and groom cut it."

She wondered if he would be able to wait that long.

"Chief Lynch!" the little boy called out as his new best friend stepped into the reception area.

The chief was focused on the wedding planner, though, and he headed in her direction. Before Rebecca could stop him, Alex took off after the older FBI agent. She would have raced after him, but he was safe—probably safer here than anywhere else.

Glass tinkled as the guests tapped silverware against water goblets. "Kiss, kiss!"

Dalton Reyes needed no encouragement to kiss his bride. He stood up and drew her to her feet. Then he dipped her over his arm as he passionately kissed her.

Jared's kisses were always full of passion. But what about love?

Feeling someone's gaze on her, she glanced up and discovered Jared standing beside her. She couldn't read the emotion in his amber eyes. But she recognized the emotion in his voice when he told her, "You got your way."

He was angry with her.

"The chief agreed?"

He grimly nodded.

And her heart began to race again with panic and fear. What had she done?

He stared so intently at her that he missed nothing. He leaned closer, so close that his lips brushed her cheek, as he said, "You can change your mind."

She shivered even as heat from his closeness warmed her. She wanted to move, just enough that his lips skimmed over hers. She needed his kiss. She needed his support. His love...

He took her hands in his—like the groom had taken the bride's as they'd spoken their heartfelt vows just a short time ago. But instead of declaring his love, Jared declared his doubt. "This is too big a risk for you and for Alex."

What about for him? Was it a risk for him? How much did he care about her?

She wanted to ask him. But she was more afraid of finding out his real feelings for her than she was of baiting a serial killer.

"You don't have to do this," he told her.

As scared as she was, she had no choice. "I have to," she said. "I have to..."

She waited for him to argue some more. But he walked away instead to take his seat at the head table, next to the groom. And then, his face revealing none of his disappointment with her reply, he toasted the bride and groom.

"When I met Dalton Reyes, he was ready to pass out just from witnessing a wedding," Jared said. "He had no intention of ever marrying. Then a short while later he found his bride—in the trunk of a car. And he started making promises he'd never made before—promises we all advised him not to make." A few other men in the room laughed. "He promised that he would find who had hurt her and that he'd stop him. And he would protect her. Dalton kept all his promises and today he made some more that he will keep just as faithfully as he kept those first promises he made to Elizabeth. And theirs will be a love that lasts forever."

Tears stung Rebecca's eyes, but she blinked them away and found Jared's gaze on her as he lifted his glass. She wanted a love like the one he'd just described. But she knew that it would never be hers—even if she lived through baiting a serial killer.

Chapter Fourteen

The diamond twinkled in the sunlight shining through the window. It was probably a couple of carats—at least. Guilt gripped Jared; he hadn't even bought Becca a ring. But then their engagement wasn't real.

Was Harris Mowery's? The woman looked more fearful than in love. So fearful that she wouldn't dare contradict her fiancé's story. She stuck to his alibi.

And the sunlight illuminated more than the diamond on her hand. It shone through the layers of makeup on her face to reveal old bruises. Jared didn't need to warn the young woman about Harris Mowery; she already knew how sadistic the bastard could be.

Like Becca, Jared wanted Mowery to be the killer. He certainly fit the profile Jared had worked up of the Butcher. But Kyle Smith's grinning face stared at him from the muted television that hung over the shiny marble fireplace in

Mowery's great room. Jared didn't need to hear what the man was saying to know that he was *reporting* the engagement of the FBI profiler to the sister of the Butcher's first victim. He wanted it to be Kyle Smith, too.

Maybe the two men were working together…

The front door creaked open, then closed with a loud slam. "Priscilla! Whose car is in the driveway?" Bristling with anger, Harris Mowery rushed into the great room as if ready to confront a lover. Then, seeing Jared, he drew to an abrupt halt and struggled to summon a grin. "Agent Bell…"

"Thought I would repay the visit you paid to Ms. Drummond's home," Jared said.

Harris's already beady eyes narrowed. "So that's what this is about? Payback?"

"That wasn't smart showing up at her house," Jared admitted.

Harris shrugged. "Thanks to your friend the reporter, everybody knows where she lives— probably even the real killer."

And that was why she was no longer at her home. She was in Jared's—her and Alex. They lived together like they were one happy family. But since she'd volunteered to bait the killer, she'd been sleeping in Alex's room instead of his. The past few days had seemed nearly as long as the past six years without her in his life.

His heart ached as if he'd already lost her. But

he hadn't. Yet. He had a couple more weeks before his *fake* wedding date. That was why he'd stepped up his investigation, hoping to break Harris's alibi. He wanted to catch the killer before the man had a chance to go after Becca.

Harris turned back to his fiancée. "Priscilla?"

The woman cringed in fear. "Yes?"

"You didn't offer Agent Bell anything to drink," he admonished her.

"Yes, she did," Jared defended the timid young woman. "I didn't want anything."

"Well," Harris said. "I would like a drink, sweetheart. Please fix me one."

She jumped up from the couch and moved to pass Harris. But he reached out for her. And she instinctively cringed in reaction. Jared jumped up, ready to defend the woman if Harris got physical with her.

But he only kissed his fiancée's cheek. "Thank you, sweetheart."

Despite the other man's sugary tone, there was a hardness in his eyes. A coldness that chilled Jared's blood. When Priscilla passed him, he reached out, too—surreptitiously—and pressed his card into her trembling hand. On the other side of that card was contact information for a women's shelter. If she didn't call him, he hoped she would at least call the shelter.

Harris waited until his fiancée was out of the room before speaking again. "But you took care of the problem Kyle Smith caused Rebecca. She's no longer staying at her house."

Jared's blood warmed now as anger coursed through him. "You went back to her house?"

"Of course not," Harris said.

But Jared didn't believe him. Harris Mowery had lost all credibility with him.

"I know she's staying with you now."

"How do you know that?" Jared asked. Was he the one who'd attacked her at the boutique, then? Whoever had must have followed her and Blaine from his apartment to the dress shop.

"You're engaged," Harris said. "So of course she would be staying with you."

They hadn't been engaged when she'd moved in, but that was none of Harris Mowery's business.

"Congratulations, by the way," the man remarked. "I'm surprised that you'd take the risk, though—what with the Bride Butcher still on the loose."

Maybe the man was too smart to fall for a trap. Even Kyle Smith had been skeptical of their announcement.

So Jared told him what he had Smith. "I already missed six years of my son's life. I should have been with him and Rebecca that whole time."

"Instead of chasing a killer?"

"Oh, no," Jared said. "I would have still chased him."

"You've been chasing him for six years, Agent Bell," Mowery said, his voice patronizing. "But you're not any closer to catching him."

Jared grinned. "Oh, I'm close now." He took a step toward Mowery. "Very close."

Harris uttered a nervous laugh and stepped back. "If you're close, you know that it's not me. I have an alibi."

"For Lexi's murder." Maybe he'd hired it done because he'd known he would be the prime suspect. "Not the others. Not Amy Wilcox's."

That anger gripped him again, flushing his face and bald head. "My fiancée—"

"Would say whatever you told her to," Jared assured him. "She didn't contradict you." She wouldn't dare.

Harris smirked. "Because it's the truth."

Jared shook his head.

"Because she loves me."

"Because she's afraid of you." She was obviously more afraid of Harris than she was of going to prison for being an accessory to murder. Jared had mentioned that threat to her. Maybe he was the one who'd made her so fearful. But he hadn't given her those bruises. He'd asked, but she'd denied having any.

"You're letting Rebecca and her wild accusations about me get to you," Harris said, and then he uttered a heavy sigh. "But of course you would, she's your fiancée now. So when's the big day?"

It would never happen if Jared had his way. Not that he didn't want to ever marry Becca. But he wanted a real wedding—not a fake one to trap a killer. "We're trying to keep the wedding small," he replied. "And private."

"So I shouldn't look for an invitation?" the man teased. "Well, I would at least like to send a gift. Where will it be held?"

"Again—trying to keep it private," Jared said. "For her protection."

"So if something happens to her," Mowery asked with that unsettling grin, "will you become the prime suspect, Agent Bell?"

Jared wanted to hit the guy. Hard.

"You wouldn't like that, would you?" Harris taunted him. "Of course I would believe you're innocent, though."

Of course he would because he knew who the real killer was: him.

"It's just so crazy to suspect the fiancé," Harris continued. "Like Rebecca suspecting me. Why? Why would I have killed my fiancée? I really *wanted* to marry Alexandra. I would still marry her today."

Priscilla, walking back into the room with his drink, paled, all the color draining from her face. Her hand, holding the glass, began to shake so much that the alcohol sloshed over the rim. Now she knew—she wasn't the woman Harris really wanted to marry.

He didn't even notice her reaction, or he noticed and didn't give a damn. He continued speaking to Jared as if she hadn't even entered the room. "Wouldn't it be more likely that the man she hadn't married was her killer?"

"What do you mean?" Jared asked. He'd interviewed the man before but he'd never brought up another suspect.

"Look into Lexi's ex-boyfriend," Harris suggested, "the man she dropped for me. That's the guy who probably killed her and, no doubt, all the others."

"Becca never mentioned Lexi having an ex-boyfriend," Jared said.

Harris shrugged. "Maybe she didn't know her sister as well as she thought she did." He grinned. "Or maybe you don't know your fiancée all that well."

"I know that no one wants to find Lexi's killer more than Becca does," he said. So much so that she was willing to risk her own life to catch him.

Harris shook his head. "She only wants her killer caught if that man is me."

"Don't you want her killer caught?" Jared asked.

The other man drew himself up taller than his stocky frame. Was his lack of height another reason he picked on women? Hurting them made him feel like a bigger man?

"Of course I want Alexandra's killer caught."

"Then why didn't *you* ever mention this ex-boyfriend before?"

Harris shrugged. "George Droski was an insignificant man. I forgot all about him."

Jared doubted that, but he wondered about Harris's timing in mentioning him. He'd had an unbreakable alibi for Lexi's disappearance. But his alibi for Amy Wilcox's abduction was shaky at best. Before he turned to head for the door, he caught Priscilla Stehouwer's gaze on him. And he suspected she might call him and the shelter.

WHILE REBECCA HAD submitted her résumé and references to a few hospitals in the area, she hadn't been asked to interview yet. Which was probably a good thing because planning her fake wedding had become a full-time job.

She cradled the phone against her shoulder as she studied the images on the computer screen in front of her. Her head began to pound and all the bright colors of the collage of wedding bouquets ran together before her eyes. "They're all beautiful, Mrs. Payne—"

"Penny, please," the wedding planner corrected her. "And you have to pick one."

Why? It wasn't a real wedding. And even if it was, Rebecca wasn't certain how interested she would be in every little detail. Lexi had tried to include her in the planning of her wedding, but Rebecca had been too busy to weigh in on any of her sister's decisions.

If only she'd given Lexi more of her attention…

"You know this isn't a real wedding," Rebecca said. The chief had assured her that the wedding planner was fully aware of the situation and the danger.

Mrs. Payne chuckled. "Yours won't be the only *not real* wedding I've had in my chapel."

"It isn't?"

"No," she replied. "But, you know, every single one of those *not real* weddings turned into *real* marriages."

"Mrs. Payne—"

"Penny," she was corrected again. "And in order for this to appear to be real, you have to pull a marriage license. So that actually makes it real, Ms. Drummond."

"Rebecca," she corrected the woman. Despite her headache, she managed a smile.

"So, Rebecca," the woman continued, "you should make all your selections based on what you'd want at your *real* wedding—because this just might wind up being exactly that."

That was damn unlikely to happen. Jared was still furious with her—so much so that he'd barely spoken to her since Dalton Reyes's wedding. Of course she hadn't given him much opportunity since she'd started sleeping in Alex's room.

She missed him. Missed lying in his arms. Missed his kisses. His caresses.

She ached for him. Not just for his lovemaking but for his companionship. If their wedding was going to be real, she would have wanted his input. He probably would have left the decisions up to her anyway, but she would have persisted until he at least offered his opinion.

She knew what his opinion was now—that she was being reckless. The pain throbbing in her head intensified. She had to squint at the pictures on her computer screen. But she made selections for the bouquet and the flowers and the cake.

"Alex will love the double chocolate," Mrs. Payne said.

The woman was sweet to have remembered her son. But then Alex—and his precocious personality—was entirely unforgettable. How well would he remember her if something happened, if the FBI agents and the bodyguards weren't able to protect her?

Now tears blurred her vision. But she blinked them back. She had to focus. She had to keep her wits about her—more so now than ever. If the agents and bodyguards didn't protect her, she would protect herself.

She wouldn't become the Butcher's next victim. And she would make certain that Amy Wilcox was his last.

"That's great," Penny said. "Your wedding will be beautiful."

If it was, it would be bittersweet: a perfect wedding with no hope of a marriage. But would she even make it to the wedding? No other bride the Butcher had targeted had made it down the aisle.

"And you'll come here to be fitted for your dress," Penny continued. Her sweet voice held no happy lilt now. It had gone flat with seriousness. She knew what Rebecca knew: that was when it would happen, when the killer would try to grab her like he had all the others. "The seamstress will come here—as well as other personnel."

FBI agents and bodyguards. They would protect her; at least Chief Lynch was convinced that they would. Jared wasn't as confident. He still thought it was too big a risk.

But Dalton's bride had been safe; nothing had happened to Elizabeth at her fitting or at the wedding. The happy couple was off on their honeymoon now.

What would Jared do if the killer didn't try to grab Rebecca at her dress fitting? Would he call off the wedding or would he see it through—to give the killer another opportunity to grab her?

Maybe she'd done all this planning for naught.

"I'm sorry," she told Mrs. Payne. "I hope this all hasn't been a waste of your time."

"Not at all," the other woman assured her. "As I said, all of the not real weddings I've held have become very real marriages." She clicked off before Rebecca could tell her that was doubtful to happen in this situation.

Jared was even angrier with her for putting herself at risk than he'd been over her keeping their son from him. She'd like to think that was because he cared about her—more than he was willing to admit. But if he really cared about her, why wouldn't he admit it—especially now if he believed he could lose her?

Rebecca was still holding the phone when it rang again. Mrs. Payne probably had another question for her—another question Rebecca would have to answer alone since Jared wanted nothing to do with their wedding.

Or with Rebecca.

He hadn't asked her to move back into his bedroom. No, he definitely wasn't in love with her.

"Yes, Penny?" she asked.

But there was no reply—just that eerie silence. She should have known it wasn't Mrs. Payne. The wedding planner was too organized to have forgotten anything.

Her hand trembling, she knew she should click off the phone. But she hadn't had any threats since that one in the boutique dressing room. It wasn't that she wanted to hear any more—just that she somehow felt as if she needed to. Maybe she could figure out who was calling her—who was watching her.

But when he spoke his voice was too low and raspy to be recognizable. "You didn't listen," he admonished her. "By getting engaged, you're risking your life."

She couldn't deny that she was—willingly—risking her life. To catch a killer...

"And now you're going to die."

Chapter Fifteen

Even with guards posted outside his apartment, the killer had still gotten to her. Anger and fear warred inside Jared, making his heart pound fast and hard.

"Doesn't this prove to you how bad of an idea our engagement is?" he asked.

Becca flinched.

Had his comment hurt her? She knew the engagement wasn't real. He couldn't really propose to her because he cared too much about her to risk her life. But when the killer was caught...

Would she want to marry him? He'd never handled anything right with Becca. He'd rejected her love six years ago. So why would she offer it again?

She shrugged and said, "It was just a phone call." As if it was nothing.

"He threatened your life," Jared reminded her of what she'd told him—of what the trace on the phone had recorded.

But even though the call had been recorded, they had no clue who'd made it. "From a burner cell," he said. Which was how all the other calls had been made. "It couldn't be traced."

She rubbed her hands over her arms as if she'd gotten a sudden chill.

Jared was chilled, too—from the threat, from the danger she was in. "It could be anyone..."

"It's Harris," she said.

"I'll have to double-check the time the call was made," he said. "I may have still been with him."

Her face brightened. "You were interrogating him again?"

"Checking his alibi," he admitted.

"I thought you did that several times already and it can't be cracked," she said.

"For Lexi's murder," he said. "I was checking for Amy Wilcox's abduction."

"His fiancée gave him an alibi?"

He nodded. While he suspected Priscilla Stehouwer might change her story, he didn't share that with Becca. He didn't want to raise her hopes—in case he was wrong. Harris's hold on Priscilla might be stronger than Jared thought.

"He gave me another suspect, though," Jared said. And now he was angry at her again for not telling him about Lexi's ex.

"Of course he did," she said. "He wants to take suspicion off himself."

"Then why didn't he give me the name six years ago?" Jared kept his voice low—because Alex was just playing in his room, but anger sharpened his tone when he added, "Why didn't you?"

"I told you who hurt my sister, but you wouldn't believe me," she said. And now there was anger in her voice. But she glanced toward Alex's room, as if afraid that he might have heard her.

"All you would talk about was Harris," he agreed. "But I asked you about other boyfriends. Exes."

She shrugged. "There was no one else—no one she ever cared enough to talk to me about like she did Harris. Not that she told me everything about Harris. If only she would have told me how he was treating her…"

"She was probably embarrassed," Jared said. Lexi had been the older sister. And Rebecca was so smart and so strong that it would have been hard for Lexi to admit what she'd probably considered a weakness on her part. Harris was the weak one.

"She shouldn't have been," Becca said. "It wasn't her fault."

"No, it wasn't," he agreed. Just like it wasn't Priscilla Stehouwer's fault. Hopefully, she at least called the shelter.

"So what name did Harris give you?" she

asked. "Who is he throwing under the bus to protect himself?"

"Lexi's ex—George Droski."

She laughed. "George was never her boyfriend. He was like a brother to us. He grew up next door to us. He was her best friend."

"Are you sure there wasn't more between them?" he asked. "He didn't have a crush on her?"

"George loved her," Becca said. "But he loved me, too."

"Harris said George was obsessed with Lexi, and that he was devastated when they broke up." As the man had walked Jared to his vehicle, he'd made certain to add to his case against George Droski.

Becca shook her head. "No. They were just friends. George didn't like Harris, though, so that had strained their friendship to the point they'd lost touch."

"Harris says he was jealous."

"He was smart," Becca said, and there was bitterness in her voice. She didn't think she'd been smart. "He realized what a jerk Harris was before anyone else did."

The pain and guilt in her voice reached inside Jared and squeezed his heart. He pulled her into his arms. "It's not your fault, either."

Now he understood why she was taking such

a big risk to catch her sister's killer—because she blamed herself.

She trembled in his arms before sliding her arms around his neck and clinging to him.

He'd missed her. Missed her being in his arms. In his bed...

A door creaked open, and Jared tensed. But it wasn't the door to the hall. It was a bedroom door.

"Family hug," Alex declared as he wedged between them.

Jared wanted to be part of this family. He wanted to be more than Alex's father; he wanted to be Becca's husband, too. But first he had to keep her alive and stop the killer who was certain to try for her again.

REBECCA KNELT BESIDE Alex's bed as she tucked him beneath the covers. He snuggled down, his eyes already closing as he drifted off to sleep. A smile curved his lips. He was happy.

And that was all a mother wanted for her child: happiness. She leaned over and pressed a kiss to his forehead. It puckered beneath her lips. And she chuckled.

He obviously didn't want her interrupting the dreams that had already begun to play through his mind.

Still on her knees, she eased back and bumped

into a hand. It covered hers and helped her to her feet. Like their son, Jared had a smile on his lips.

But she didn't believe he was happy. He was too angry with her. When she met his gaze, though, she didn't see any anger in his eyes. She saw only desire—desire that brought out her own desire for him.

"He's asleep," Jared said. He'd read him a story before going to check with the guards in the hall. "And everything's quiet outside."

It wasn't quiet inside her. Emotions were rioting in her heart. She loved him so much.

He turned toward the door, but his hand was still around hers. He tugged her along behind him. When they cleared the threshold, he reached around her and closed their son's door. His chest bumped against hers, and he stared down at her, those amber eyes intense with desire.

"What are you doing?" she asked.

"Bringing you to bed…"

She pointed at the door he'd closed. "I've been sleeping in there."

But he headed away from that door, across the living room to the master bedroom on the other side of the apartment. "And you should have been sleeping in here."

"Why's that?" she asked as he led her into his bedroom.

"Because it's where you belong," he replied as he pushed the door closed. "With me."

Just in his bed? Or in his life?

If she were braver, she would have asked. But it seemed to be easier for her to face a killer than Jared's feelings for her. Because if he didn't feel the same…

She couldn't handle him rejecting her again.

He wasn't rejecting her now. He was quickly disrobing her with hands that shook with his urgency and his passion. Then he was kissing her with all that passion.

Her heart began a frantic beat. His tongue slid between her lips and teased hers. She gasped, and he deepened the kiss even more.

Then she was fumbling with his clothes, her hands shaking as she unbuttoned buttons and unsnapped snaps. Then she jerked down his zipper.

He groaned. Then he murmured her name. It was only a few steps, but he carried her to the bed and followed her down onto it. The rest of their clothes disappeared until there was only skin sliding over skin.

Heat burned inside her as pressure built and wound tighter and tighter. He kissed her everywhere. Her lips. Her throat. Her breasts.

He slid his lips along the curve and across her nipple. Then he drew the point between his lips and teased it with his tongue.

She wriggled beneath him as that pressure

became unbearable. She needed him too much to wait. It had been too long. "Jared..."

And she touched him. She knew exactly where would drive him crazy. His chest. His lean hips. And lower...

"Becca!" His control snapped, and he was inside her—where she needed him most. Sliding deep, filling her.

She wrapped her legs around his waist and clung to him, meeting every thrust. He kissed her deeply, sliding his tongue into her mouth.

Her body shuddered as pleasure overwhelmed her. If he hadn't been kissing her, she might have screamed. Or declared her love.

Like the pleasure, love overwhelmed her.

Then he joined her in ecstasy, his body tensing as his pleasure filled her. He rolled to his side and clasped her closely in his arms. His heart beat hard and fast against hers. And he murmured her name, "Becca..."

She tipped her chin up to meet his gaze. His pale brown eyes were full of intensity. It couldn't be desire again—not so soon.

And he murmured her name again as if he was going to say more—as if he was going to express whatever intense emotion burned in his gaze.

But the doorbell rang.

Rebecca could have cursed. But he beat her to it. Then he reached for the cell phone he'd placed, along with his weapon, on the table next to the bed. He glanced at the blank screen and shook his head.

"What is it?" she asked. She shivered, maybe because he wasn't holding her anymore, maybe because she had an ominous feeling.

"The guard at the door is supposed to call me," he said, "not ring the bell." He vaulted out of the bed, pulled on his pants and reached for his weapon.

Before she could say anything—warn him to be careful—he was gone, closing the bedroom door behind him. She couldn't stay in the room. Not if he was in danger. Not if their son might be in danger, as well.

She grabbed her robe, thrust her arms through the sleeves and cinched the belt at her waist. Then she hurried into the living room.

Jared stood in the open doorway, his gun drawn. But there was no person standing in the hall. Not the guard. Not a killer. He was looking down, though, so Becca followed his gaze and saw the box.

"What is it?" she asked.

He held out his arm as if holding her back. "Don't come any closer."

Fear quickened her pulse. "What do you think it is?" She glanced across the living room to their son's bedroom doorway. "Is it ticking?"

He leaned down and listened, then shook his head. "This serial killer has never used a bomb."

She shivered. "No."

"It would be too quick for him," Jared said, almost as if he was thinking aloud. "Too impersonal."

"So what's in the box?"

"Get back," he told her as he lifted his weapon again.

Maybe the box was only a distraction, so that someone could sneak up while they were staring at it. But she recognized the voice of the guard as he said, "Agent Bell, I'm sorry—I thought I heard something in the stairwell. It sounded like someone might have fallen. I know I should have called you before I went to investigate. But I was worried that someone was hurt…"

"It's okay," Jared assured the other man. "That was the distraction, so someone could leave this box."

Rebecca stepped closer to get a better look at the box. It was wrapped in shiny silver paper, and there was a bow on the floor beside it—like it had fallen off.

"It's a present," she said. "A wedding present."

For their fake wedding.

"It's a message," Jared said. "He knows where you are…"

"He already knew," she said. "Whatever's in the box is the message."

"Do you have gloves?" Jared asked the guard. He wouldn't want to compromise any evidence.

But Rebecca doubted there would be any inside the box. It was another threat. Another warning that she would die. But she stepped even closer as Jared donned the gloves and reached for the lid of the box.

He lifted it easily and peered inside.

"What is it?" the guard was just as curious as Rebecca. "And what's on it?"

Lace spilled from the box like lace had spilled from the trunk of Lexi's car when they'd found it. This lace wasn't stained red, though. Whatever was on it was darker and dried.

"It's a veil," Rebecca said. Just that afternoon she'd flipped through images Penny Payne had sent her of veils, like she'd sent the bouquet and cake pictures.

"A wedding veil?" the guard asked.

She nodded. Then she waited until Jared looked at her. When his gaze was on hers, she told him what she really thought. "It's Lexi's veil."

Chapter Sixteen

Other women had been murdered. The veil could have belonged to one of them. Lexi's wasn't the only veil that hadn't been found. But not all of the women had intended to wear them with their gowns.

Would Becca?

Jared didn't want their fake wedding to get that far, though—far enough that she was fitted for her gown. He needed to catch the killer first. But the next suspect he wanted to interview was proving difficult.

"I need you to come into the Chicago Bureau," Jared told the man over the phone. He was at the Bureau now—restlessly prowling his office as he waited for the lab to get back to him about that veil.

"I don't understand why you need to speak to me, Agent Bell," George Droski replied.

"It's about Lexi Drummond."

A soft sigh rattled the phone. "I haven't thought about Lexi in years…"

That didn't make him sound as obsessed as Harris Mowery had claimed he was.

"Not even when you've seen the news about other women being murdered just like she was?" Jared asked. It would only be natural to think about her then.

A heavier sigh rattled the phone. "I guess I've thought about her then."

"Another woman was just murdered."

"I saw that on the news," George admitted.

But was that the only way he'd learned about it? Or had he killed Amy like he'd killed all the others?

"Had you ever met her before?"

After a hesitation, George asked, "Who?"

"Amy Wilcox."

Another hesitation and then he said, "How would I have ever met her?"

"She was a friend of Lexi's." Or so Becca thought.

"That was a long time ago," George said. "A lot has happened since I saw Lexi last. I got married. I have two daughters. I really don't remember much about back then. I think my coming in to the Bureau would just be a waste of your time, Agent Bell."

Jared silently agreed, and he realized why Harris Mowery had mentioned George as a suspect. He'd wanted Jared to waste his time on a dead-end lead instead of pursuing a real suspect: him.

"I'd still like to talk to you," Jared persisted. He needed to meet the man in person to assess if George Droski could fit the profile he'd done of the Butcher. "If you won't come in, I'll come out to meet you."

There was another hesitation. Or maybe the man's cell phone just had poor reception. Then George replied, "I'm sure I can get to your office soon. I'll check my schedule and call you back."

Since Jared didn't have any evidence to link Droski to any of the murders, he couldn't justify having him picked up for questioning.

"I will expect a call and a meeting soon," Jared warned him. Because if the man tried to avoid meeting with him, then maybe he had something to hide. He clicked off the phone as his office door rattled with a knock.

He glanced up, hoping the lab tech had brought the results from the veil. But it wasn't a tech. He opened the door and greeted the man, "Mr. Kotlarz…"

Amy Wilcox's fiancé looked as if he hadn't slept since she'd first disappeared. A twinge of guilt struck Jared for thinking that the man had cared more about the engagement ring he'd given his fiancée than he'd actually cared about his fiancée.

"Agent Bell," the man's tone was sharp with anger and disapproval. "I'm surprised to find you here. Thought you were too busy getting engaged to work Amy's case."

He'd obviously seen Kyle Smith's news broadcasts.

"I am still very much working the case," Jared assured him.

"Do you have any new leads?"

Another person, a lower-level agent, stepped into Jared's office with an envelope. "The lab results, Agent Bell," the young woman told him. "I know you were waiting for these."

"Thank you," Jared said.

She smiled and turned to leave. And Troy Kotlarz watched her walk away. Maybe he didn't look so tired because he'd been grieving.

Jared tore open the envelope.

"Are those lab results from Amy's crime scene?" Troy asked. "Did it take all this time to get them back?"

"No," Jared said. "We got those back already."

"And you didn't call me?"

"There was nothing to report," Jared said. "Nothing to lead us to Amy's killer."

"And what about the ring?" Troy asked.

Jared should have counted how many minutes it had taken the man to ask about his family heirloom. Maybe it was all he cared about, and he'd only asked the other questions so he didn't appear callous.

Jared shook his head. "I'm sorry. It hasn't turned up yet."

Unable to wait until the man left, he pulled the lab results out of the envelope he'd already opened. The report confirmed that the stain on the veil was blood. Lexi Drummond's blood.

Becca had been right.

"Have you been checking pawnshops?" Troy asked.

"No," Jared said. "We're looking for a killer—not a thief."

"But if he pawned the ring, it could help you find him," Troy suggested.

Jared nearly laughed. Kotlarz was totally unaware of his profile of the Butcher. "He wouldn't pawn the ring."

The color drained from the brawny man's face. "What are you saying? That he's keeping it? It's some kind of sick souvenir for him?"

Jared nodded.

Serial killers often kept souvenirs, mementoes to remind them and help them relive their kills. The Bride Butcher had always kept something related to the wedding. Veils. Shoes. In Lexi's case, her veil and her body.

"So I'll never get the ring back then," Troy said, his broad shoulders slumping with dejection.

Had he already had someone else picked out to give it to?

Before Jared could ask, the man walked out. Jared didn't expect to see him again—now that he'd given up hope of finding his grandmother's ring.

The chief passed him on his way out and gave him a curious glance. "Amy Wilcox's fiancé?"

Jared nodded.

"Was he putting pressure on you to find her killer?"

"That wasn't his primary concern," Jared replied.

"Agent Munson said you had the lab results."

Jared handed them over.

The chief rubbed a hand over his chin. "This should make you feel better about your engagement."

"Better?" The bloodied veil was a message to Becca—that she would wind up like her sister if she tried to get married. "This proves how dangerous this is. We need to call off the engagement." His next call would be to Kyle Smith—to give him an exclusive on his broken engagement.

Lynch slapped the report down onto Jared's desk. "You were just given new evidence on a six-year-old case. This is the most progress you've made in a while."

"Progress?" he scoffed. "This does nothing to lead us to the killer."

"You don't have to chase the killer anymore," Lynch said. "You have him coming to you now."

Jared shook his head. "Not to me—to Becca."

"We will keep her safe," the chief vowed. "Rebecca Drummond is the key to you finally catching the killer."

He wanted to catch the killer, but not if it meant losing Becca.

REBECCA SQUINTED AGAINST the lights as she stepped out of the doors of Alex's school. Agent Campbell held tightly to her arm; whenever they were out now, he kept close to her side. He blinked against the flashing bulbs of the cameras.

The press had ambushed them—the same way they had ambushed Jared at her house that first time she'd seen him in six years. And like then, Kyle Smith led them like the alpha leading a pack of wild dogs.

He thrust a microphone into her face. "Ms. Drummond, do you really expect us to believe your engagement is real?"

Blaine tugged Rebecca away from the reporter. But Kyle followed, keeping the mike in her face. "Back off," Agent Campbell warned him.

"It's okay," Rebecca told her protector. She wanted to talk to the reporter. "I want to answer his questions."

"Of course," Kyle said. "Because you want to use me and the rest of the media in order for you and Special Agent Jared Bell to set your trap for the Butcher."

She blinked as if stunned by his accusation even as her heart pounded frantically with fear that the plan had been blown. It would never work now. She drew in a breath to steady herself and replied with a question of her own, "Do you think that the FBI would use a civilian to bait a killer?"

She had him stunned because he shot no question back at her.

"They would never risk my safety," she said.

"But Special Agent Bell would," Smith replied with his usual animosity for Jared.

"He would risk the life of the mother of his child?" she asked. "You don't know Jared at all."

"By putting a ring on your finger, he's risking your life," Smith argued.

But Rebecca wore no ring. Fortunately, she'd pulled on her gloves before she'd stepped outside, so Kyle couldn't know her hand was bare—unless he looked closely. She slid her hands into her pockets.

"I will be safe," she said and hoped like hell that she spoke the truth. "I wouldn't have accepted Jared's proposal if I didn't believe he could keep me safe."

Except that Jared had never proposed and probably never would even if she survived their fake engagement.

The reporter smirked. "Come on, Ms. Drummond. I think you would do anything to catch your sister's killer."

Maybe the man knew her better than she'd realized.

"I leave catching criminals to my fiancé," she replied. "I'm too busy planning my wedding to the man I love."

"You love him?" the reporter scoffed.

She nodded. "We've been apart for too long. You know we share a son. And we don't want to wait a minute longer to become a real family."

If only that were true…

"So you're serious—your engagement is real?" the reporter persisted.

She drew in another breath and looked directly into the camera. "I am in love with Jared Bell," she said, and realized that she spoke the truth. "I've been in love with Jared for six years."

Blaine glanced at her and nodded. Either he approved of how she was handling the obnoxious reporter or he approved of her loving his friend.

"So something good came of your sister's death then," the reporter said, as if trying to justify Lexi's murder.

Had Jared been right to suspect the reporter could be more involved than she'd thought? Had she been entirely too focused on Harris Mowery to the point that she hadn't realized there could have been another killer and Lexi was just a random victim?

"I wish Jared and I had met some other way," she said. Because then he never would have doubted her feelings the way he had six years ago. "But I'm glad that we met. And I can't wait to become his wife."

"Do you really think that the Butcher will ever allow that to happen?" Smith asked, almost as if he pitied her.

She kept her reply to herself and allowed Blaine to escort her through the throng of reporters. But no, she didn't think that the Butcher would let her make it to the altar.

Chapter Seventeen

The way she stared into the camera as she vowed her love made Jared feel as if she was speaking directly to him. But that declaration wasn't meant for him; it was meant for her sister's killer. So that the Butcher wouldn't suspect she was setting a trap for him.

Kyle Smith had suspected it was a trap. Was he the killer?

Jared cleared his throat and gestured at the television. "You were convincing," he told her. His heart ached with longing. He wished she'd been speaking the truth, that she really loved him. But if she loved him, why had she kept their son from him?

Sure, he'd rejected her earlier declarations of love. He'd thought her feelings couldn't be real then—not with everything else she'd been going through. When she hadn't contacted him about Alex, she'd proved him right. Hadn't she?

While he sat on the couch in front of the TV,

she was in the kitchen, putting away the leftovers from the dinner she'd made. Alex was reading in his room. It was like they were already married; like they were already a family. He wished that were true, too.

She shrugged. "I don't know if I was convincing enough."

"I guess we'll know soon." Her dress fitting was scheduled in a couple of days. If the Butcher followed his previous pattern, that was when he would try to abduct her.

Try. That was all he would be allowed. An attempt. He wouldn't take her as he had all those other women. Jared would make certain of that.

"I almost hope you're right," she remarked.

"About?"

"Kyle Smith," she said. "I almost hope it's him."

"Harris Mowery's wrong about you," Jared said. "He's convinced he's the only suspect you'll consider."

She snorted derisively. "I'm not going to consider George a suspect." She pointed at the television. "But Kyle Smith…" She shuddered. "It was like he was using our relationship to justify Lexi's murder."

"I caught that, too," he said. But it had been hard to focus on anything but Becca's declaration of love. "I'm still working on finding links between him and any of the victims."

"But do serial killers have to have a link to their victims?" she asked. "Or do they just randomly choose them?"

"Usually there's a link to one of the victims," he said. "The first one."

"Lexi…" She shook her head. "She didn't know Kyle Smith." She stepped away from the kitchen to join him near the couch. But she didn't sit down beside him; she didn't touch him. She didn't act like a woman in love—even though she was back to sharing his bed. "It must be Harris Mowery."

"Or it could be George Droski…"

She shook her head. "Not a chance."

"Or maybe there was a victim before Lexi…"

Her blue eyes widened with shock. "Do you think so?"

"I haven't found another death that matches the Butcher's MO," he admitted. "But there are a lot of missing persons cases."

"So, maybe, like Lexi, his first victim was never found?"

"It's something I'm looking into—if Kyle Smith knew someone who disappeared before Lexi."

She drew closer to him now and knelt before where he sat on the couch. She slid her palm over the side of his face and said, "I'm sorry."

She'd already apologized—several times—over not telling him about Alex. "Why?"

"I hope you never think I doubted how hard you've worked on this case," she said. "I hope you know how much I appreciate how hard you've worked."

He had worked hard. Maybe that was one of the reasons he'd rejected her declaration of love six years ago—because he'd wanted to focus on finding her sister's killer. He'd known she needed that more than she'd needed him.

And he'd denied how much he needed her. He leaned over so that his lips touched hers, sliding back and forth in a gentle kiss.

Her breath escaped in a wistful sigh.

He would have deepened the kiss, but the doorbell rang—like it had the other night.

She tensed. "Who would ring the bell?"

She knew that the signal was a phone call to announce an intruder or a visitor. Jared reached for his weapon, and she sprang to her feet and headed to their son's bedroom—to protect him.

Jared needed to protect them both. His weapon in his hand, he approached the door. And like the night they'd found the bloody veil, he opened the door to another ominous present. But there wasn't just one—there was a pile of them.

"WHERE DID THEY come from?" Rebecca asked as she saw the assortment of different-sized boxes wrapped in shiny paper. "Did someone sneak them up here?"

Jared shook his head. "No, they were delivered to the front desk."

"Then you'll be able to get a description of who dropped them off," she said and expelled a breath of relief. "You'll be able to find him." And stop him.

Jared sighed, too, but with resignation. "These were all deliveries. The presents were mailed here."

"From where?"

He glanced down at the boxes he'd taken from the doorman who'd brought them up from the lobby. He'd dropped them at the door when the guard had grabbed and frisked him. "Several different places."

"But we're not registered. We haven't even sent out invitations to this wedding." Because it wasn't real. "So why would anyone send us gifts?"

He shrugged but opened one of the cards attached to a present. "To Rebecca Drummond, you've been through so much with losing your sister. You truly deserve your happiness."

She took the card he held out and read the signature. "I don't know this person."

"But maybe she thinks she knows you—from the news coverage," he said. "Maybe Kyle Smith gave out your address again."

Or they'd tracked her down through him. Kyle had given out his name, too. But she looked at all the boxes and shivered. What if the gifts weren't as innocuous as the card? What if they contained other macabre gifts like the bloodied veil?

Despite her telling him to stay in his room, Alex's door creaked open, and then he bounded into the room with a shout of excitement. "Look at all the presents! It's not my birthday, though. Or Christmas…"

He looked up at his father. "It's not Mommy's birthday, either. Is it yours?"

Jared shook his head. "Nope, my birthday is in April."

"Then why are there so many presents?"

Jared looked at Rebecca now. "With the news coverage, he's bound to find out…"

"Find out what?" Alex asked.

Jared was right. They couldn't keep him reading or playing in his room all the time. He went to school. He would eventually overhear something.

She drew in a deep breath and turned toward their son. "People think your father and I are getting married."

His blue eyes brightened and a big smile creased his little face. "That's—"

"But we're not really getting married," she hastened to add. "We're only letting people think that we are."

"Why?" he asked. But she suspected it was

more than his natural inquisitiveness that had him asking questions.

"Because it's going to help catch the bad guy who took away your aunt Lexi," she said. "Remember how I said I was going to help? This is how I'm helping."

"No," he said. "I meant why aren't you getting married for real?"

Pain clutched her heart. She wished the wedding would be real. She wanted it to be real. "You know that not all mommies and daddies are married."

He had friends with divorced parents.

He nodded. "But those mommies and daddies don't love each other anymore."

And he thought they did? Maybe he'd overheard the television replaying the impromptu interview she'd given Kyle Smith.

She opened her mouth but she had no words. She couldn't deny her feelings for Jared. She did love him. And she wouldn't lie to her son.

"We have to catch this bad guy before we can do anything else," Jared spoke for her.

Alex nodded as if he completely understood.

Rebecca wished that she did. Was Jared implying that something could happen after the bad guy was caught? That he might actually propose then? Or was he only putting off Alex's inevitable disappointment?

She had a feeling that she would be even more disappointed than their son.

His eyes still bright with excitement, he moved closer to the presents Jared had piled onto the coffee table. He asked, "Are these gifts real?"

Nerves fluttered in her stomach as she remembered finding that veil stained dark brown with old blood—with Lexi's blood. What else of Lexi could be inside those boxes? Her body had never been found.

"Alex," she cautioned as she reached for him. "You really shouldn't touch them."

"So they're not real…" Alex uttered a soft little sigh of disappointment.

"We're not sure what they are," Jared said. "We need to get them checked out before anyone opens them."

"How?" Alex asked.

"I'm going to have an agent pick them up and bring them down to the Bureau," Jared said. "They'll x-ray them there."

The little boy giggled. "Like Mommy x-rays people to check for broken bones?"

Jared smiled. "Yes, like that."

"When is the agent coming?" she asked.

"He'll be here soon," Jared assured her.

Rebecca breathed a sigh of relief. She would be glad when the presents were gone.

Alex stepped a little closer to the coffee table. "That one's so pretty," he mused. And as he pointed, the small brightly wrapped present, piled on the others, toppled down onto the floor.

As it had the other night, the cover fell off the box and the contents spilled out. The box was too small for anything too gruesome or frightening.

But, like the veil, Rebecca immediately recognized the sapphire-and-pearl earrings that bounced across the hardwood. Her hands shaking, she leaned over to pick them up.

"That present was real, Mommy," Alex said. "And they're pretty."

And like Lexi, Rebecca had thought they were gone forever. That she would never see them again...

"There's a note, Mommy," Alex said as he reached down for the box.

"No," Jared told him, then softened his sharp tone and continued, "don't touch that. We might need to check it for fingerprints."

Alex nodded. "Yeah, fingerprints...but Mommy is touching the earrings. Won't she mess up the fingerprints?"

"Yeah," Jared said. "Let me talk to Mommy alone a minute while you pick out a bedtime story in your room."

Her son brushed past her on his way to his bedroom. But she couldn't take her gaze from the jewelry cradled in her palm. She was aware, though, that Jared moved, that he leaned down and picked up the note he'd told their son not to touch.

"What does it say?" she asked him.

Instead of answering her question, Jared asked one of his own, "What are they? You must recognize them or you wouldn't be staring at them like that."

She shivered. "They were Lexi's something blue…" Their grandmother had given them to her.

"I'm sorry," he murmured. "I shouldn't have brought the gifts inside the apartment. I should have had the agent pick them up from the front desk."

She curled her fingers protectively around the earrings. She wouldn't have wanted anyone else touching her family heirloom.

"What does the note say?" she asked again.

He reached out and squeezed her shoulder. "Becca…"

She wanted to lean into the warmth and strength of his hand. Or turn and burrow into his arms, seeking comfort and protection. But Jared had warned her that the fake engagement would put her in more danger, and she'd ignored his advice. She'd told him she could handle it. So she stiffened her spine and prepared to handle it.

"I already know it's another threat," she said. That was all she received lately—either through phone calls or dressing room visits or cruel *gifts*. "Just read it to me."

He sighed but he recited the words he must have memorized since he didn't even look at the note. "Something borrowed. Something blue…"

He hesitated. And she knew there was more to it than that.

"Jared…"

"Don't go through with the wedding," he continued, "or you'll be dead, too."

Chapter Eighteen

He found her in his bed. But she wasn't sleeping. She jumped when he pushed the door fully open and stepped into his bedroom. "It's just me," he said. "I didn't think you'd still be awake."

He wasn't sure if he would find her in his bed, either. He'd had to invite her every night—after they tucked their son into his bed. But Jared had left before Alex's bedtime.

"What did you find out?" she asked.

"The other boxes held just gifts," Jared assured her.

"Are you sure?" she asked. "Maybe I should have opened them because I would recognize anything that belonged to Lexi."

"If it had belonged to Lexi," he said, "there would have been some not-so-cryptic note included. There were no more notes like that one."

She expelled a shaky little breath.

"One note was more than enough," he said. It had shaken her. And it had shaken him, too.

"More than enough to convince you that I'm right—that it's too dangerous to go through with this fake wedding."

She shook her head. "I was getting threats before we even got *engaged*. Someone grabbed me before we got *engaged*."

"But let you go because you weren't engaged," he pointed out. "That dress fitting is coming up in a couple of days. We need to call this off." Because he couldn't risk losing her.

"I still won't be safe," she said, her voice vibrating deep in her throat, but not with fear— with anger. "I won't be safe and neither will any engaged woman in the country until the Butcher is stopped."

He couldn't argue with her. For one, he was too damn tired. So tired that he stripped off his clothes and climbed into bed with her. And for another, she was right; nobody was safe until the Butcher was caught.

So he drew her against him and held her. He could keep her safe here—in his arms. He wished she could stay there forever, pressed tightly against his heart that filled with love for her. But he couldn't tell her of that love now; he could barely acknowledge the feelings himself. He had to focus instead on protecting her.

"We'll find another way to catch him," Jared said, "without putting your life at risk."

She settled against his chest with a soft sigh.

But he knew it wasn't resignation. She wouldn't give up, which she confirmed when she said, "He's gone free too long. He's hurt too many people. This is the fastest way to catch him."

And the fastest way for Jared and Alex to lose her. He tightened his arms around her. He wouldn't let her go. "Then I'll protect you," he promised. "I'll make sure nothing happens to you."

For their son's sake but mostly for his.

Now her breath shuddered out in a sigh of relief that caressed his chest. Then her lips slid over his skin.

And he wasn't tired any longer as his pulse began to race and his heart hammer. He tipped up her chin and kissed her with all the passion burning inside him. While he didn't want to tell her how he felt about her, he set out to show her. He made love to her tenderly and slowly—kissing and caressing every inch of her silky skin.

She moaned and writhed and cried out as pleasure overwhelmed her. But it wasn't enough. He wanted to give her more. He made love to her with his fingers and his mouth and his tongue.

But she wanted more. She reached down and wrapped her hand around him, stroking him to madness. His control snapped, and he thrust inside her—into her heat and warmth. She wrapped her legs around his waist and arched into his every thrust. They moved in perfect rhythm. And together, staring deeply into each other's eyes, they came apart—their sanity and hearts lost as they found ecstasy.

The words filled his throat then—the declaration of love he wanted to give her. He had to give her...

But it would only complicate things further, and they were already complicated enough. So he swallowed his words and settled her against his chest again, against his heart, and wrapped his arms tightly and protectively around her.

And he hoped he could keep the promise he'd made her—that he could make sure nothing happened to her. He had to keep her safe.

REBECCA AWOKE ALONE the next morning. Maybe Jared was only in the kitchen or playing with Alex. But the apartment felt emptier than that. It felt like he was gone.

She felt like he was gone—because there was an emptiness in her, too. He'd promised to protect her, so there was probably a guard or two at the door. Or maybe one of his friends, a special agent, ready to follow her wherever she wanted to go. She had no doubt that Jared was trying to keep his promise to protect her—by finding the killer before she was in any danger.

But then he could be putting himself in danger. He'd interviewed so many suspects that he must have talked to the killer—more than once.

If the Butcher suspected he was getting close, he might stop Jared before Jared could stop him.

Despite the warmth of the bed, she shivered. Then a phone rang, and she jumped. Maybe it was Jared, though, so she grabbed up her cell from the bedside table. "Hello?"

And her heart sank at that ominous hesitation. But after a few seconds, it wasn't the raspy voice that spoke to her. It was a familiar one. "Becca?"

"George?" She hadn't heard from her childhood friend in years. Six to be exact. He'd called and expressed his concern for her when Lexi had disappeared. How could Jared have ever suspected him? "Is everything all right?"

"Yes," he replied. "I think so…"

"What's wrong?" she asked.

"An FBI agent called me a couple of days ago," he said. "He wants me to come to the Chicago office for an interview. Do you know if I'm actually considered a suspect?"

"George, I don't know." Could Jared really consider him a suspect?

"It's the agent—the one I've heard on the news that you're engaged to," he said with an emotional crack in his voice. He was hurt.

Kyle Smith had made sure that news report had gone national—she wasn't even sure where George lived since he'd moved away from their hometown in Ohio.

"I'm sorry," she said.

"I didn't know if you were the one who mentioned my name to Agent Bell…"

"It wasn't me," she assured him. "I don't believe you had anything to do with Lexi's murder. I know you would never hurt her."

"I would never hurt her," he agreed.

"It was Harris Mowery," she said. "He's the one who told Jared about you."

"Mowery?" He cursed. "Of course it was him."

Jared most definitely had interviewed the killer—when he'd interviewed Mowery. "I know it's him," she said. "He was the one who hurt her."

"He's the reason Lexi's gone," George said. "I'm sorry, Becca…"

She shivered again—at his strange apology. "Why, George?"

"I shouldn't have called you."

"I'm not sure why you did," she admitted. She hadn't heard from him in six years. "You don't have any reason to be concerned about Jared interviewing you."

Or did he?

"It's just strange," he said, "being questioned in her disappearance, especially after all this time."

"Jared is just being thorough," she said. "He won't arrest anyone without evidence." No matter how much she'd wanted him to put Harris

Mowery behind bars for the rest of his miserable life.

Instead, the man was engaged—going to get married—probably going to have children. He was doing all the things he'd robbed Lexi of when he'd taken her life.

"I know," George said. "It's just strange. But I really called for another reason."

"What's that?" Rebecca asked.

"Aren't congratulations in order?"

She'd known George too long to lie to him. So she said nothing.

"You are getting married, right?" he asked. "That's what all the news reports are saying."

She didn't know if she would actually make it to the altar or not. Jared had promised to protect her, not marry her. But she needed to say something, so she repeated what she'd told Kyle Smith. "I love Jared Bell very much."

"You must," George said, "since you're risking your life to marry him."

She sucked in a breath of shock at his comment.

"I'm sorry, Becca," he said. "I'm just repeating what that slimy reporter's been saying—that that sick killer will probably go after you."

"I'll be safe," she assured him and herself. Chief Lynch had promised her, and now so had Jared.

"I hope so," George said. "I really wish you all the best, Becca."

"Thanks," she said. But she wasn't sure what else to say to him beyond, "Goodbye." She ended the call with an uneasy feeling twisting her stomach into knots.

George's call had been strange. She doubted he'd called to offer his congratulations. Was he really worried about Jared interviewing him?

Why?

She couldn't believe he had anything to do with Lexi's death. He'd been like a brother to them. Maybe that was why he'd called—because he was genuinely concerned for her safety.

So was Jared.

He didn't understand that she wasn't just doing this for Lexi and the Butcher's other victims and potential victims. She was doing this for him, too. He needed to catch the one killer who eluded him. The Butcher was his white whale—the one who'd hurt his otherwise spotless career, the one who caused Jared great guilt with every new victim the killer claimed.

She had to do this. For him...

That was how much she loved him.

The phone rang again, and she breathed a sigh of relief. It had to be him. "Yes?" she answered it.

But there was that ominous pause. And then that raspy voice asked, "Are you getting the message yet? Have you canceled the wedding?"

She tensed, but instead of fear, anger coursed

through her. She was done playing the victim to this monster—done with the sick games. "Absolutely not."

"Then you're going to die."

The line clicked dead…like she would soon be if the caller's ominous prediction came true.

Chapter Nineteen

"You didn't have to come back early from your honeymoon for this," Jared told Dalton Reyes. But he was damn glad he had. He'd seen first-hand how fiercely Reyes had protected Elizabeth when she'd been in danger. The former gang-banger had the street smarts to help keep Becca safe.

And Jared needed all the help he could get. His stomach knotted with dread. Her dress fitting was only hours away.

Reyes smacked his shoulder. "You had my back," he reminded Jared. "Now I've got yours."

"It's not my back I'm worried about," he murmured as Becca walked into the living room after closing the door to Alex's bedroom.

With her hair caught up in a high ponytail, she looked younger than her nearly thirty years. She looked like a teenager. Too young and too vulnerable to face a killer. But as she stepped closer, he saw the resolve and determination on her beautiful but pale face. He also saw the moisture of tears in her eyes. Saying goodbye to their son had affected her. Was she worried that it might've been her last time?

Unconcerned that Reyes watched them, he pulled her into his arms. "I will protect you," he promised. He would make damn sure she saw their son again.

Fortunately their son was safe; Blaine Campbell was in his room, probably hooked up to the lie detector test with the list of questions Maggie Campbell had given the little boy to ask her husband. Blaine would protect their son with his life.

Jared had good friends. And he'd never needed them more than he did now.

Becca clung to him for just a moment before pulling back. Tilting up her chin, she said, "Let's do this."

He wanted to kiss her—wanted to bring her back to bed and make love to her. Just in case it was the last time...

Not for her, though. She would be safe. He intended to confront the killer before the man could get to her.

"You'll ride up with Reyes," he said.

"Not you?"

Because of all the tension, he tried for humor. "Isn't it bad luck for the groom to see the bride's gown before the wedding?"

But instead of smiling, her face grew even

paler. His joke had fallen short. But then he'd never been funny.

"The killer will know it's a trap," Reyes said, "if Jared drives up with you."

Becca nodded. "Of course."

"I'll keep you safe," he promised again.

"And so will I," Reyes assured her.

"You can change your mind, though," Jared reminded her. "You don't have to do this." But he'd already seen the grim determination on her face. He knew she wasn't changing her mind even before she shook her head.

She swung a bag over her shoulder and spoke to Reyes. "Let's go."

"Everything's in place at the chapel," he updated Reyes. Undercover agents and bodyguards were hidden all over the place. The killer would not get to her.

Reyes nodded. "We're going to get him."

She turned back to Jared. "And it won't be George Droski."

She didn't sound as confident as she once had, though. She'd told him about the man's phone call that had unsettled her.

But the guy had come to Chicago for that interview. He'd been nervous. Nervous enough to make Jared nervous.

"It'll be Harris Mowery," she insisted.

Jared wasn't so sure. Some alibis had fallen apart but not for Harris Mowery.

He walked out with them, but when their car pulled out of the parking garage, he didn't follow. He turned toward another section of town— a higher-rent district—and found a parking spot on the street near Kyle Smith's building.

Since the guy hadn't been parked outside Jared's building the way he usually was, Jared wondered if he'd already left for the chapel. He would have found out when Becca's dress fitting was; he would have made a point of it.

Penny Payne had confirmed a break-in of the office in her wedding chapel/reception hall. And the organized woman was certain someone had gone through her date book. Jared was pretty sure that had been to find the time for Becca's fitting. He wouldn't have cared about the wedding. Nobody expected her to actually make it to the altar.

Least of all Jared. Once they caught the killer, the fake wedding would be called off. Unless he could convince her to forgive him for how he'd treated her six years ago.

Maybe she already had. But had she forgiven him enough to let herself love him?

He would find out—once the killer was caught. He stepped out of the car and swung the door shut. And as he headed into the lobby, he patted his jacket, making sure his gun was ready. Not that he would have forgotten it today.

Today was the day he needed it most. To protect the woman he loved. He flashed his badge at the doorman. "I need to see Kyle Smith."

The doorman picked up the phone. "He's not answering, sir."

"Did you see him leave?"

Had he already beat Jared to the dress fitting at the Little White Wedding Chapel?

The doorman shook his head. "No, and he didn't call for a car."

"I need to go up to his apartment," Jared said.

"Agent Bell…"

The doorman obviously recognized him—thanks to Kyle Smith. "You know he'd want to see me," Jared said. "He's usually parked outside my apartment." Or following Becca everywhere she went.

Why hadn't he called for a car?

The doorman leaned closer and whispered the reporter's apartment number. Then he winked. Apparently he wasn't any more a fan of Kyle Smith than Jared was.

"Thanks," he said as he hurried into a waiting elevator. The doorman had given him the apartment number, but Jared probably should have asked for a passkey, as well. Kyle Smith probably wouldn't be in a hurry to open the door for him—especially if he'd learned that some of his alibis had fallen apart.

Of course the reporter had struggled to remember where he'd been when each woman had disappeared, so he might have inadvertently given Jared incorrect information. Or he might have slipped up.

Finally. Six years later…

Jared paced the elevator car as it ascended. Maybe he should have taken the stairs. But finally it stopped with a sharp jerk. Long seconds passed before the doors began to slide open. Jared didn't wait for them to open all the way; he squeezed through the first crack in the doors and headed down the hall.

Hell, if Smith refused to let him in, Jared would just break down his door. Giving incorrect information in a federal investigation gave Jared the right to bring him in for further questioning.

But he didn't have to break down the door; it gaped open. Had the doorman had a change of heart and alerted Smith? Jared swallowed a curse. But then he noticed the broken doorjamb. Smith hadn't done that running out; someone had broken in. He reached for his gun and pulled it from the holster beneath his jacket.

He pushed the door fully open and stepped inside. Furniture had been overturned and pictures had been knocked off the walls. He moved slowly through the apartment, stepping over things until he came upon the body.

Kyle Smith stared up at him, but for once he didn't wear that smug grin. His mouth was open, blood trickling from the corner and over the side of his face. And his eyes were open, too, staring blindly.

He was dead. He wasn't the killer, but maybe he'd figured it out. Maybe he'd found the evidence that Jared had been looking for all these years, and that was why his apartment was torn apart. The killer had been looking for it.

Why hadn't Smith called him? Had he been saving the reveal for a special news broadcast? Probably. And trying to further his career had cost Kyle Smith his life.

Jared uttered a sigh, but the breath had barely passed his lips when he heard a creak. Maybe it was just some of the broken furniture. But before he could turn, something struck his head—hard.

Pain blinded him, and his knees folded from the force of the blow. And he fell beside Kyle Smith. But he didn't have to look into the dead man's face for long—because everything went black as oblivion claimed Jared. He only had time for one final thought: he'd broken his promise to Becca. He wasn't going to be able to keep her safe.

SPECIAL AGENT NICK RUS leaned in the open driver's side window. He wore a hard hat and looked like a road crew worker holding up traffic with a sign. "I don't think you should go on to the chapel until Jared gets here."

Dalton glanced over at Rebecca as if debating how much to reveal in front of her. Then he replied to Rus, "Jared was stopping somewhere to check out another lead before meeting us here."

"Did he bring backup with him?" Rus asked, his blue eyes darkening with concern.

Rebecca's pulse had already been racing with fear for herself—for what she might encounter in that dress fitting room. A monster. But now she worried about Jared. Was he facing the monster now?

"Where was he going?" she asked.

Dalton shrugged. "All he would say is that he was following up on an alibi that had fallen apart."

A gasp slipped through Rebecca's lips. "Harris. He had to be going to see Harris Mowery."

"Why wouldn't he say?" Dalton asked.

"He probably didn't want to get my hopes up," she suggested. Six years ago she'd been relentless in wanting him to arrest her sister's fiancé.

Dalton pulled out his cell phone and punched in a number. He muttered a curse before saying, "It went straight to voice mail."

Agent Rus glanced at the backed-up traffic, as if looking for Jared's car. "He wouldn't miss this."

"No, he wouldn't," Dalton Reyes agreed.

Her heart pounded harder and faster. "Do you think something has happened to him?"

Dalton shook his head. "No. He wouldn't have risked being late for your fitting."

"No," she said, "unless he thought he could catch the killer before…"

"The killer catches you," Dalton finished for her.

Her fear increased. "But what if the killer caught him?"

Dalton and Rus both shook their heads. "Jared's a better field agent than he even knows. He's fine."

Were they lying to her so she wouldn't worry? Or was Jared the one playing games? Maybe he thought if he didn't show, the fitting would get called off. Was that his way of protecting her— to get the whole operation canceled?

The only way to truly protect her and countless other women was to catch the killer. If Jared had apprehended the Butcher, he would have called.

She drew in a deep breath to brace herself. "It's getting late," Rebecca said. "We need to do this."

Rus shook his head, then cursed.

"Lynch in your head?" Dalton asked.

Rus touched his earpiece and nodded. "The boss says to proceed. We have enough backup without Jared."

Chief Lynch must have come to the same conclusion Rebecca had—that Jared hadn't showed because he had never approved of setting a trap using her as bait. Anger replaced her fear for him. And that anger strengthened her resolve.

"Let's do this."

Rus stepped back from the car and waved them through to the church. Dalton parked at the curb and escorted her up the stairs. But he wasn't the only one in the area. A lawn care crew worked on the grounds around the church. One mowed while another trimmed shrubs and a third worked a weed eater.

Even if he didn't realize they were special agents and bodyguards, she doubted the killer would try to grab her with so many people around. Jared hadn't needed to worry about her. But apparently he wasn't worried or he would have showed up.

She hurried up the steps to the church as if anxious for her fitting. As if she couldn't wait to marry the man she loved.

And she did love him—despite how frustrating and stubborn he could be. But she doubted that they would ever marry. Mrs. Payne greeted her in the foyer—with a big hug.

"I remember you from Dalton's wedding," Penny Payne said. And she reached up and patted the special agent's cheek like he was a small boy. "Such a handsome groom he was. And his bride…"

"Beautiful," Dalton said with a loving smile.

"You will be a beautiful bride, too," Penny promised her. "I bet you can't wait until you see your dress…"

Rebecca couldn't wait until this was over and she could return to her son. At least Blaine Campbell was protecting him. Alex was safe. With the list of questions he'd had to ask Agent Campbell, he was also occupied and amused.

"The dressing room is right this way," Penny said as she led Rebecca to a short hallway off the foyer.

A door stood open and inside the sunny-yellow room was a tall, dark-haired woman. She had a measuring tape draped around her neck. But Rebecca recognized her from the wedding. She was one of the bodyguards.

"This is my seamstress," Penny said. "Candace…"

The other woman smiled at Rebecca. "Your dress is in the garment bag. Please try it on, and we'll see where we need to make adjustments." With Penny Payne, she stepped out of the room and closed the door—leaving Rebecca alone inside.

But she wasn't alone. She had a mike taped onto her, so that Dalton and every other FBI agent in the area could hear her call for help—if she needed it. She suspected she wouldn't need it.

Obviously, Candace had made sure the room

was empty before she'd shut her inside. So what was she supposed to do now? Try on a dress that she would never wear anyway?

She reached for the zipper of the garment bag, but just as she began to pull it down the door opened again. She drew in an unsteady breath, but it was only Candace again.

"Are you okay?" the bodyguard asked.

"Of course," Rebecca said. "Why wouldn't I be?"

"The perimeter guards caught someone trying to get in through a basement window," Candace replied.

Rebecca started forward, but Candace blocked the doorway. "Stay here," she advised her. "Until I make sure the suspect's been contained."

Goose bumps lifted on Rebecca's arms. She wasn't sure they'd contained the actual suspect. It was probably just Kyle Smith who'd been trying to break in to get exclusive coverage of her murder.

But before she could voice her concerns to the female bodyguard, Candace closed the door, once again shutting Rebecca alone in the room.

But when she turned around, Rebecca realized she wasn't alone any longer. Someone else stood inside the room with her—someone she'd never suspected.

A scream burned her throat, but she was too shocked to utter it. Too shocked to do anything to save herself…

Chapter Twenty

Jared winced when Reyes touched the back of his head. "You probably have another concussion," the agent said. "You should've gone to the hospital instead of driving up here."

But he'd promised Becca that he would protect her. He hadn't done a very damn good job of that, though—at least not personally.

"We had this," Nick told him. "You should have gone to the hospital. What the hell happened to you?"

"Kyle Smith's dead," he revealed.

Dalton whistled. "I know the guy was a pain in your ass, but I didn't think you'd actually kill him."

"I found him dead."

"So how'd you get the blow to your head?" Dalton asked. "Trip over his body?"

Jared winced as he remembered nearly falling on the dead man. "I didn't realize the killer hadn't left yet."

"You must have been out for a while," Reyes remarked, "since he beat you here."

Jared touched his head himself. While the blow had caught him by surprise, it hadn't been as damaging as the one he'd taken while protecting Elizabeth. Sure, he'd lost consciousness, but he hadn't thought he'd been out that long.

"It's probably good he was in a hurry," Reyes said as he touched Jared's wound again. "Or he might have finished you off like he had Kyle Smith. Why do you think he killed Smith? Do you think the reporter figured out who the killer was before we did?"

Jared didn't even know who the killer was. "Where is the suspect?" he asked.

Reyes chuckled. "Does it irritate you that we caught him without you?"

"I just wanted him caught," Jared said. He followed Reyes over to one of the Bureau's black SUVs. The windows were tinted, so he couldn't see inside. "Open the door."

Reyes clicked the locks and gestured at the handle. "I'll let you do the honors."

Jared pulled open the door and expelled a breath of surprise. Becca was going to be horribly disappointed that her trap had snagged the person she'd least suspected.

"It was hard to get you to come up to Chicago," he said. "Surprised to see you came all the way up here. From… Where is it you're from again, Mr. Droski?"

The man said nothing.

So Jared answered for him. "You're from St. Louis, George. Did you forget? But then you're a very busy man—busy with your wife and kids. Or busy abducting and killing brides-to-be?"

"And apparently knocking federal agents over the head," Reyes added for him.

George Droski ignored Reyes but focused his gaze on Jared. During the interview the man hadn't been able to look him in the eye. Instead, he'd stared down at the table between them. The guy had red hair—not Jared's auburn—but a fiery red. He also had freckles and pale skin. He was nobody's image of what the Butcher would look like; he looked like Howdy Doody, not a violent serial killer. "It's not what you think…"

And the nerves he'd shown during their earlier interview were gone. It was almost as if he was relieved.

Serial killers often said that they'd wanted to be caught—after they were caught. That they were hoping that someone would stop them. As a profiler, Jared knew that was bullshit and just a feeble attempt for the killer to save face. They got caught when they got cocky—when they'd gotten away with their crimes for so long that they believed they couldn't be caught.

But he didn't believe George Droski was

trying to save face. The man didn't have the arrogant, narcissist personality that Jared had profiled the Butcher would have.

He shook his head. "It's not him."

Dalton laughed. "Just because you didn't catch him?"

"It's not him," Jared repeated as he turned and headed toward the church. He was vaulting up the steps when he heard Becca scream—a scream of pure terror. Other agents started forward, as well, but Jared shook his head. He wanted to assess the situation first—to make sure Becca hadn't been taken.

George Droski was talking now—drawing the attention of the agents away from Becca's scream to him. But Jared didn't care what he was saying. He cared only about Becca.

His weapon drawn, he rushed through the doors and toward the room from where the scream had emanated. Hoping he wasn't too late, he kicked open that door. Becca wasn't gone—not like all those other brides-to-be.

She was pale and shaking with her hand clasped over her mouth. There was no blood. No wounds. But she looked horrified—as shocked as if she'd seen a ghost.

"Are you okay?" he asked. "What's wrong?" Then he turned and saw her, too. The ghost. The woman whose murder he'd spent six years trying to solve.

"No wonder I never found your body," he mused. "Hello, Lexi."

JARED SAW HER, TOO. She wasn't a ghost. Or a figment of Rebecca's imagination. She hadn't lost her mind. And apparently she hadn't lost her sister—at least not the way she'd thought she had these past six years.

And anger replaced her shock and fear. "Why?" she asked and her voice cracked. She refused to acknowledge the tears burning her eyes. Her voice had cracked because of the scream—the one she hadn't even realized had slipped out. She had stood there for so long, just staring at that apparition—because certainly it couldn't have been real. Lexi couldn't be real. But Jared saw her, too.

She cleared her throat and asked again, "Why?"

And for the first time since she'd unzipped the garment bag and stepped out, Lexi spoke. "I'm sorry…"

It wasn't enough. Rebecca shook her head. "I'm not looking for an apology. I want a reason—a reason that you put me through hell." All the pain and guilt and regret…

And the loss. That horrible ache of emptiness that Rebecca hadn't been able to fill—not with love for Jared. Not even with love for her son.

"Answer her," Jared ordered.

Tears filled Lexi's bright blue eyes. She looked the same, exactly the same as she had six years ago. That was why it had been almost easier to believe she was a ghost than to believe she was real. And that she'd chosen to leave.

"I had no choice," Lexi said. "It was the only way I could get away from Harris. Or he really would have killed me. I'm sure he's been killing those other women." She shivered, and the tears overflowed her eyes and slid down her beautiful face.

Rebecca had missed her sister so much. All she wanted to do was pull her into a hug and hold her. And introduce her to Alex.

But there was so much she didn't know yet. "How?" she asked. "How did you do it?"

"There was so much blood," Jared added. "The coroner said you couldn't have lost that much blood and lived."

"As well as being a medical assistant, I'm also a phlebotomist," Lexi said. "I was taking small amounts of my blood for a couple of months and freezing it."

Jared nodded. He had known about Lexi's certification. But who would have believed she had used that skill to draw so much of her own blood? Not Rebecca. She was horrified. "You planned it for a while…"

And she'd never said anything to Rebecca. While she should have been thrilled her sister was alive, she still felt as if she'd lost her. Or maybe she'd never really had her at all.

"I'm sorry," Lexi said again as the tears continued to stream down her face. "But I wasn't sure you would go along with it. And I had to get away from Harris."

"You could have just dumped him," Jared suggested.

Lexi shook her head. "I tried. He nearly killed me then. And he promised me that was the only way I would get away from him—was when I died." She uttered a ragged sigh of resignation. "So I had to die."

Rebecca had seen the bruises. She knew her sister spoke the truth. That was why she'd been so convinced that Harris had killed Lexi—because he would've had Lexi given him the chance. Instead, she'd saved herself the only way she'd known how.

"Is that who the agents caught outside? Was it Harris?" she asked Jared. "Or was it Kyle Smith?" She wouldn't have put it past the reporter to try to break into the chapel for another exclusive.

"Kyle Smith is dead," Jared said.

She noticed then the grimness on his handsome face and the streak of blood on the side of his neck. "Are you okay?" she asked. Had he fought with Smith? Had he been right that was who the killer was?

"I'm fine," he said. But the grimness didn't ease, and he still held his gun, the barrel pointed at Lexi—as if she posed some kind of threat. "And the person who was caught outside the chapel is George Droski."

"George?" Rebecca asked. "I was so sure he had nothing to do with the killings. He was so close to us growing up—like a brother."

"Maybe he was like your brother," Lexi said. "But he was never like mine."

Rebecca wondered about her sister's tone. She'd been even closer to George than Rebecca had. "But you two were so close…"

"We're closer now," Lexi said, and she smiled through her tears. "We're married."

"Married?" She'd thought Lexi had been robbed of her wedding, of her life. It was so hard to believe that she'd been living the past six years.

"He saved my life six years ago," Lexi defended the man, "when he helped me escape from Harris. George would never hurt anyone. He's only been helping me—trying to save you, too."

Rebecca's stomach churned as she had another revelation about her sister. "You were the one behind the warnings?"

"Of course it was her," Jared said. "Who else would have had the veil with her blood on it? And your grandmother's earrings?"

"Her killer," Rebecca murmured. She'd been so convinced that was who had been playing the mind games with her. But Lexi had done it. She'd never really known her sister at all.

"It must've been George calling you," Jared said. "And George who tried to grab you in the dress boutique."

"Why?" Rebecca asked her sister again. She'd always thought that Alex got his inquisitiveness from Jared. But maybe he'd gotten it from her.

"Because you are in danger," Lexi said. "Kyle Smith was making too big a deal out of you, making you too tempting a target for Harris to pass up. And I know he was going to try to kill you—especially after he killed Root Beer."

"Amy Wilcox?" Jared asked.

Lexi nodded. "That had to have been Harris. He only met her once, but he hated her."

"He has an alibi," Jared said.

Lexi snorted. "I'm sure he does. But it's not true."

"You're the expert on what's not true," Jared said. "You admit you faked your own death and terrorized your sister."

Lexi flinched as if Jared had struck her.

Rebecca loved them both. And she understood them both. Lexi had felt as if she'd had no other way out. But Jared had to be angry that he'd spent six years trying to solve a murder that had never been committed.

But then Jared pulled out his handcuffs. "Lexi Drummond-Droski, I am placing you under arrest for obstruction and harassment."

Rebecca gasped. "You can't!" Anger was one thing, but this felt vindictive. And she'd never thought Jared could be vindictive. He'd forgiven her for not telling him about his son. Hadn't he?

"I have to," he told Rebecca as he snapped the cuffs around Lexi's thin wrists. "She's broken the law. And the ones I'm arresting her for might not be the only crimes she and George have committed."

He wasn't making any sense. Maybe the blood on his neck had come from a blow to the head—one that had addled his thinking. "What are you talking about?"

"She faked her death," Jared said, "but all those other women are *really* dead. We found their bodies. And the way they died exactly fits the way we thought she had died."

But of course they had thought that only after those other bodies had been found—with all those horrible stab wounds. Then it had made sense that they'd found so much of Lexi's blood if she'd also been stabbed.

But she'd stabbed herself—over and over again—with a needle. She'd been that desperate to get away from Harris. Lexi looked tiny standing in front of Jared—little bigger than

Alex. Putting the cuffs on her was like arresting a child—someone vulnerable and innocent.

Rebecca shook her head. "Jared, you're not making any sense…"

"He thinks I killed them," Lexi said.

"You and your husband," Jared said. "It had to be you and George. He abducted the women like he tried to abduct Becca in that dress boutique."

"He wasn't trying to abduct her," Lexi argued. "He just wanted to scare her so that she wouldn't get any more involved with you and risk her life."

Jared's chin snapped up as if she'd struck him. "You think I'm a danger to Becca?"

"You broke her heart six years ago," Lexi said. "And you put her at risk today. I got in here. George nearly got in here. Harris could have, too."

"I think you're the greater danger," Jared said. "Harris doesn't know every detail about your crime scene. You do because you staged it. And all those other crime scenes exactly match it. It has to be you and George who killed those other women."

"I didn't know those other women," Lexi said. "I only knew Amy, and I never would have hurt her."

"Like you didn't hurt your sister?" Jared asked. "You've been terrorizing her—"

More tears ran down Lexi's face. "I didn't mean to—I just wanted her to be careful. To protect herself—"

"But this wasn't the first time you hurt her," Jared said. "You nearly destroyed her six years ago."

"I'm not sure which one of you hurt me more six years ago," Rebecca said. It was as if they were having a contest, but the loser would be the one who'd hurt her most. "But you're hurting me now, Jared. I just found out Lexi is alive, and you're taking her away…" Her voice cracked with emotion. "In handcuffs."

He looked at her, his amber eyes full of regret. She noticed the dark shadows beneath his eyes and how a muscle twitched in his cheek. He was in pain. He must have been hurt earlier; that was why he hadn't shown up when he'd promised. And she'd thought he was just trying to stop her from putting herself in danger.

"I have to," Jared said. "She can't get away with what she's done."

"No, she can't," another man agreed as he stepped through the open door of the dressing room. He slammed it shut behind himself. At first Rebecca thought it was the crack of the door hitting the jamb that she heard.

But it was too loud, so loud that she winced. Then she screamed as she saw Jared crumple and drop to the floor. And she turned back toward the other man. Harris Mowery held a gun—a gun he'd just fired at the man she loved.

Chapter Twenty-One

Jared lay limply on the floor, blood trickling down his numb arm and soaking through his shirt and coat to the carpet beneath him. The bullet had missed his damn vest, hitting his shoulder instead. He'd dropped his gun. And because he'd dropped his gun, he'd dropped to the ground, too.

With a wounded arm and probably a concussion from what he suspected was now an earlier confrontation with Harris, he wouldn't be able to physically overpower him. He needed his gun. And he had to get it without Mowery noticing him reaching for it. He had to play dead and hope that Mowery didn't fire at him again.

He also had to get a message to his team so they didn't rush the room and force Mowery's hand. Because then he would definitely empty his gun—into Becca and Lexi before they'd have a chance to take him down.

Rebecca's scream had drawn Mowery's attention to her, so the man had turned away from him. But the gun had fallen too far away for Jared to reach for it quickly—without drawing Mowery's attention back to him. With his left hand, he pulled his badge from beneath him and flashed it at the stained-glass window.

He didn't flash an SOS. And because he hadn't, Rus and Reyes should know to back off and hold back the others. And let him handle it. As long as Harris didn't realize he wasn't dead...

"You shot him!" Becca yelled at Harris as she tried to move around him. But he swung that gun in her direction. "Why did you shoot him?"

"So he wouldn't try to save you," Harris said. "I needed Special Agent Bell out of my way. And you better stay where you are, Rebecca, or I'll shoot you, too. And that isn't at all what I've had planned for you."

Jared knew what he'd planned. The same gruesome death as all those other women but Lexi had suffered.

"What are you doing?" Becca asked.

The madman chuckled. "You knew I wouldn't be able to resist grabbing you, Rebecca. That was the whole purpose of your little plan. Kyle Smith was right about that..." He sighed almost regretfully. "I don't know why he resisted giving up the information about your fitting time and location. I knew he had it. And he'd always been so good about sharing his information before—until today."

"You killed him," Becca said, and her voice cracked with fear and with tears. She was probably worried that he'd killed Jared, too.

"I would've killed Special Agent Bell then, too," Harris said. "But I needed him to lead me back here. Back to you…" He swung his gun toward Lexi. "I didn't know he'd lead me to you, as well."

"You're not surprised I'm alive," Lexi said.

Clearly, Harris hadn't been as shocked as he and Becca had been.

"You're not going to be alive much longer," Harris promised her. "But first I intend to take care of your sister. She's been a pain in my ass for far too long."

He swung the gun toward Becca but Lexi lurched forward—stepping between them. She glanced down and noticed Jared staring up at her. And she shook her head in warning just before Harris turned back toward him.

So Jared closed his eyes and played dead, like Lexi had the past six years.

"How did you know I wasn't dead?" she asked, her voice, which had been so soft earlier, was loud and shrill now. She wanted to draw Harris's attention to her. And away from Jared.

She was helping him.

"I knew because I hadn't killed you," he said.

"But I did—every time I killed one of those women. I killed you. I saw you—especially when I killed that insolent girl we met at the mall."

Lexi gasped. "Root Beer…"

"Whatever you called her," Harris said. "You and your childish little nicknames."

"Do you know what I called you?" Lexi asked.

"I never let you give me one of your ridiculous pet names," he said, his voice full of patronization and pride.

She smiled—a smile full of his usual smugness and arrogance. She was playing him hard, hitting all of his triggers.

For Becca…

To keep her sister safe from the man she'd brought into their lives.

"I had a nickname for you," Lexi told him. "I called you the Little Man." She laughed. "For so many reasons…"

He lashed out—just as she'd intended, striking her so hard that she dropped to her knees. "You bitch! You stupid little bitch!"

He raised his arm again to deliver another blow.

Lexi couldn't defend herself. She couldn't even lift her arm to deflect his blow because Jared had handcuffed her arms behind her back.

Jared reached for his gun, out of reflex with his right arm. But the numbness wasn't gone. It was like he was paralyzed. He couldn't move the limb that had been shot. He couldn't save Lexi from the next blow Harris dealt her.

But Becca could. With another scream, this one of anger instead of fear, she threw herself at the madman. Maybe she'd forgotten about his gun. Or maybe she was just so angry that she didn't care.

Another shot rang out, rattling the small stained-glass window in the room. Had Harris shot her?

PAIN EXPLODED IN Rebecca's head. The bullet hadn't struck her, but the barrel had when Harris swung it at her. The force of the blow made her fall to the ground next to Lexi. She'd only wanted to protect her sister—like she should have six years ago.

"And that's one of the reasons you're a little man," Lexi said. Blood oozed from the cut he'd opened on her lip. But she didn't care. She kept taunting him.

It was obvious to Rebecca that Lexi wanted him to kill her first—before he had a chance to kill Rebecca. Despite letting her believe she'd been dead the past six years, Lexi still loved her—enough to die for her. "Stop," she implored her. "Don't…"

"Don't what?" Lexi asked. "Tell the truth? I should have gone on that dead reporter's show years ago—telling what a weak, little man Harris Mowery is. That he can only pick on women."

"I killed that reporter," Harris said with pride. "I beat the dress fitting time out of him."

"I thought you said he wouldn't tell you," Rebecca reminded him. "That you had to follow Jared here."

He swung his gun back toward Jared. "I killed him, too. Or if he's not dead now, he soon will be." He pointed his barrel at Jared's head.

And Rebecca screamed. The hope that he was only unconscious was what had kept her from losing her sanity. If Jared was dead...

She would lose more than her heart. She would lose her mind and her soul, too. "No!" She vaulted to her feet and launched herself at Harris again.

But another shot rang out. She didn't know if it struck Jared or the floor near his head. She had no time to look—no time to go to him—before Harris tossed her back onto the ground like a rag doll.

She hit with a hard thud, jarring her bones and bruising her muscles. An oath slipped through her lips.

And Lexi screamed now. "Stop! Stop hurting her!"

"I'm going to do more than hurt her," Harris promised.

"I'm the one you want to hurt," Lexi said. "I'm the one you hate."

Harris cursed—calling his former fiancée every vulgar name a man could call a woman. "But you're wrong," he said. "I don't hate you. Not even now."

Lexi shivered. Maybe she would have preferred his hatred.

"I love you," he said, then cursed her again. "I love you like I've never loved anyone else…"

And Lexi had rejected him. She'd rejected life entirely over a life with him.

"You don't know what love is," Lexi said. "You have no idea."

"And you know?" he said with a snide smile. "Are you talking about your love for your sister? You put your darling *Becca* through hell when you faked your death."

Lexi shook her head. "I love," she said, "my husband. My children."

Harris's face flushed red with rage. Lexi had pushed him too far. He was certain to kill her now. "You're married?"

"Yes," she replied with a happy smile that made her swollen lip bleed even more. "And we have two beautiful children."

He lashed out again—so quickly that he struck Lexi before Rebecca could intervene. Lexi fell back on the floor. Then Harris swung the gun barrel toward her. "Don't move."

"Don't shoot her!" Rebecca yelled. She couldn't lose Lexi again—especially not if she had already lost Jared. She would need Lexi to hold her together.

"I'm not going to kill her yet," Harris said. "I want her alive to watch when I kill you." He turned back to Rebecca. But he slid the gun into the back of his belt. And instead he pulled out a knife and unsheathed it. "Of course she doesn't love you as much as her husband and children." He flicked his thumb over the shiny blade of the sharp knife. "I really should kill them instead..."

He shook his head. "But that would be breaking with my MO." He turned back to Lexi. "You know it," he said. "You gave it to me."

"How?" she asked. "How did you know exactly what happened there?"

He smiled again—that arrogant, smug smile. "Kyle Smith had a mole inside the Bureau. Some stupid female agent that fell for his slick smile—she kept him apprised of all the details of the case."

"And he told you?" Rebecca asked.

"Not intentionally," Harris said. "Probably not even consciously. He was a fool. And a braggart. It was easy to play him for everything he knew."

Except this last time. Kyle must have figured out he'd been aiding a killer, and he hadn't wanted to help anymore.

Why hadn't help arrived for Rebecca? There

had been agents all around earlier. Had they left to bring George to jail? Poor innocent George who would lose the mother of his children if Harris had his way.

The agents must have left, or they would have heard this conversation through the mike she wore. They would have come to her aid and Jared's. Instead, he was bleeding to death on the floor. And as Harris swung that knife toward her, Rebecca realized that she would soon be bleeding, too.

She lifted her hands, but she didn't know how she would be able to fight off that blade. That sharp blade that had already killed so many other women.

"No!" she screamed as that knife slashed through the air on its descent toward her chest. Her heart...

Chapter Twenty-Two

Jared was right-handed, but with that arm numb and bleeding, he had to use his left hand to grab for and fire his weapon. So he squeezed the trigger and emptied the magazine, hoping that he hit the son of a bitch.

Harris's body tensed as at least one bullet struck him. But he didn't drop the knife, he clutched it harder as he lunged down on Becca.

Screaming filled the room. But it was Lexi—not Becca. She just lay still—beneath Harris's still body. Had Jared been too late to save her?

He cursed himself—furious that this killer had gotten the jump on him twice. And now he might have killed the only woman Jared had ever loved...

He lurched across the short space separating him from their tangled bodies. With one arm, he dragged Harris off her. He'd had to drop the gun. If the guy held the knife and was still alive, he could plunge that knife into Jared's heart. But if he'd already killed Becca, Jared had no heart left to hurt. And Harris had no life left to take anyone else's. His limp body slumped onto the floor, and he stared up at Jared through eyes wide with shock and fury.

He'd died knowing that he'd failed. He hadn't killed the woman he'd wanted to kill. He hadn't killed Lexi Drummond. She scrambled to her knees, tears streaming down her face. Together they moved toward Becca.

Her eyes were open, too, and wide with shock. Her hands clasped her stomach. Jared cursed, and Lexi gasped. But then he noted that no blood oozed between her fingers. Instead of being plunged in her body, the knife was stuck in the floor next to her arm.

He had missed. Not only had he died but he'd died without taking either Becca or Lexi with him. Jared should have felt relief or even triumph. But his heart hadn't stopped pounding with fear for Becca's safety.

"Are you okay?" he asked her. He had to touch her, so he slid his fingers along her cheek. She was so beautiful but so pale and fearful. "Becca?"

Her breath shuddered out in a sigh of relief. "You're alive. I was so afraid that he'd killed you."

"I was afraid for you," he said. "And you..." He turned to Lexi. He shouldn't have cuffed her;

he'd made her helpless to defend herself. But that hadn't stopped her from defending and trying to protect her younger sister.

He needed to find the key to the cuffs. But he couldn't take his good hand from Becca's beautiful face.

But then the door to the dressing room opened and he pulled his hand back to reach for his gun.

"You didn't flash SOS," Rus said as he stepped inside with his gun drawn.

"That's because I had this," Jared said.

"You just flashed once, so I knew you were alive," Rus said. "We held back because—"

"He would have shot us all if you'd tried breaking through the door," Jared said.

"We heard it all," Dalton added. "Rebecca was wearing a mike."

"So you released my husband?" Lexi asked.

"We caught him trying to break in," Dalton said. "And we heard what you and he did to your sister."

Jared pulled out the key to his cuffs and handed it to Dalton. "Let her go. She was just trying to protect her sister."

"But she faked her death," Rus added.

Jared stared down at the body of the dead man. Then his gaze went to the huge knife shoved deep into the floor. "To escape the Butcher..."

He didn't blame Lexi for what she'd done.

He blamed himself. He should have listened to Becca. He'd gotten hung up on Harris having an alibi for Lexi's abduction, so he hadn't looked at him as a suspect in the other murders like he should have. If he had, he could have saved some of the other women. Harris had had no connection to them, though. He'd randomly picked brides—probably from their engagement notices in the paper—and as he'd killed them, he'd imagined Lexi. If Jared had caught Harris earlier, Lexi would have been able to come home to her sister and the rest of her family. It was more his fault than Lexi's that she'd had to stay away so long. "I'm sorry," he told her.

Dalton unhooked her, and she pulled her arms in front of her and rubbed her wrists. "I understand why you would arrest me," she said. "You must be furious over what I did."

"I understand why you had to," he said. "And that's why I'm sorry. I failed you. I should have caught him a long time ago. So you could have come home."

Tears spilled out of Lexi's eyes. "It wasn't your fault. None of it was."

She might see it that way, but he doubted that Becca did. Would she ever forgive him for not listening to her? And even if she could, he wasn't certain that he could forgive himself.

"We need to get you to the hospital," Nick

said. "You should have gone after you took the blow to the head. Now you've been shot…"

Maybe it was the head wound or the loss of blood from the gunshot wound or maybe it was just hearing Rus say it aloud, but Jared suddenly got very dizzy. His vision blurred, and the pain in his head and shoulder intensified. He groaned, then dropped as oblivion claimed him again.

HER HEART POUNDING and nerves frayed raw, Rebecca paced the hospital waiting room. She'd nearly lost Jared so many times in just a few hours. He couldn't have saved her life only to leave her life. Tears blurred her vision. She loved him so much. Alex loved him so much.

Her little boy couldn't lose his father now—when he'd only just learned who he was. That was her fault. It was all her fault.

She hadn't let Jared know about his son. And then she'd committed to that crazy plan to flush out a killer. She was a physician's assistant, not an FBI agent. She hadn't been prepared for anything that had happened.

"I could help him," she murmured. "I should have helped him at the scene. I could have stopped the bleeding…"

"Harris wouldn't let you near him," Lexi reminded her. "He would have shot you, too."

She shuddered as she remembered how close

she'd come to being Harris Mowery's latest and last victim. She had felt the air move from the slash of that sharp knife. If Jared hadn't shot him...

Lexi stepped into the path of her pacing. When Rebecca moved to the side, Lexi matched her movement and caught her. Then she pulled her into her arms and hugged her. Rebecca held herself stiffly. If she gave in to the tears, she probably would never stop crying.

But she felt Lexi's tears dampening her shirt and her skin as she clutched her closely. And Rebecca found her arms lifting and wrapping around her sister. She hugged her back. She was real. She was warm and soft and real. She was alive. And the tears began to fall.

"I'm sorry," Lexi murmured. "I'm so sorry..."

At first Rebecca thought she was offering the kind of apology people offered at funerals as an expression of sympathy. But Jared couldn't be dead. He couldn't...

She pulled back from her sister and looked around the waiting room. His friends were there—but for Blaine who'd stayed with Alex. Instead of pacing like her, they stood in a corner—talking and laughing. Trading stories about Jared.

They knew him better than she did. He'd been part of her life such a short time—six years ago—and a short time now. He couldn't leave her. But even if he survived his wounds, he would still probably leave her. The killer was caught now—dead now.

She trusted that he would stay part of Alex's life. But what about hers?

"He has to be okay," she murmured.

"He is," Lexi said. "He was so focused on saving you. He won't leave you."

"He did," Rebecca said, pain cracking her voice. "He left me six years ago. He didn't think I really loved him. He thought I was just using him to get over losing you." Tears threatened again, but she blinked them back. "But I never got over you."

"The news has been reporting that your son is his," Lexi said. "I have a nephew…"

"Yes, Alex," Rebecca said, and her heart warmed with love for her amazing child. "But I didn't tell Jared when I got pregnant. He just recently found out that he's a father."

"So I'm not the only Drummond who kept a secret for years," she said. "Do you hate me for what I put you through?"

"No," Rebecca said, and she pulled her sister back into a hug. "I could never hate you. I'm so glad you're alive. Were you telling the truth— do you and George have kids, too?"

Lexi smiled again and reopened the wound on her lip. "Two girls. Becky is five, and Amanda is three." She blinked back tears. "The same years apart that we are. I think they'll be as close as we were."

"Why didn't you tell me?" Becca asked. "Why didn't you tell me what a monster Harris was?"

"He would have killed you," Lexi said. "I worried that he still would when you kept publicly accusing him. That's why George and I have kept an eye on you all these years. I've seen Alex…" Her voice cracked with emotion. "I can't wait to meet him, though. And I can't wait for you to meet my girls."

All Rebecca had wanted the past six years was to have her sister back—to share her life the way she wished they'd been doing before Lexi disappeared. But she couldn't think about her now. She couldn't think about anyone or anything but Jared.

"He has to be okay," she murmured again.

The door to the waiting room opened, and a doctor stepped inside. It was the ER doctor who'd treated Jared. She rushed forward—along with Nick Rus and Dalton Reyes, who asked, "How is he?"

"He'll be fine," the doctor assured them. "We did a CT scan. He has a slight concussion."

"What about the gunshot wound?" Rebecca asked.

"The bullet went through his shoulder," the

doctor replied. "He needed a few stitches and an IV. He'll be fine. Would you like to see him?"

Rebecca stepped back as the agents stepped forward. They turned to her. "You can go first," Nick Rus offered.

She shook her head. "No, that's okay. I'm sure he'll want to talk to you about the case. He'll want to get everything finished up." She stepped back again—until she bumped into Lexi.

Lexi's hands gripped her shoulders and steadied her. The agents left—anxious to see their friend. And instead of holding her, Lexi shook her, albeit gently. "What are you doing?" she asked. "You want to see him. You've been so worried about him. Why didn't you go see him?"

Rebecca shook her head. "I don't know…"

"You know," Lexi said. "Tell me."

"Because it's over," she said. "Harris is dead. The Butcher has been stopped. It's over."

"The killing is over," Lexi agreed. "My having to play dead is over. But you and Jared—that doesn't have to be over."

"It was just an act," Rebecca said. "A trap. We never intended to get married."

Lexi uttered a soft sigh of disappointment. "So Jared was right six years ago. You didn't really love him."

Self-righteousness filled Rebecca. "No, he wasn't right. I did love him. I really loved him.

It had nothing to do with filling any void you'd left. It was about him. I loved him."

"'Loved'?" Lexi asked. "Past tense? You don't love him anymore?"

"No…" If anything, she loved him more. He was such a good man. Such a good father for only just finding out that he was one. He and Alex had a bond—in their genius—that she would never share. But it was more than that. They were close already.

And Rebecca had seen what their life could be like as a family, taking care of and playing with Alex together. And then she and Jared sleeping together every night, wrapped up in each other's arms.

"So you don't love him anymore," Lexi said.

"I didn't say that," Rebecca said. She wouldn't lie to her sister. She wouldn't lie about her feelings for Jared.

"So you do love him?"

Maybe Alex had gotten his inquisitiveness from his aunt. "Why do you keep asking? Why do you care?"

"Because I want to know," Lexi said. "You willingly used yourself as bait for a serial killer. So I thought you were brave, but you're acting like a coward now—when it comes to admitting your feelings."

"I want to know, too," a male voice added.

She turned around to find Jared standing

behind her. Even though the doctor hadn't said anything about discharging him yet, Jared was dressed already—in his bloodied shirt and coat. And she was more afraid of facing him than she'd been of facing the serial killer.

What if she admitted her feelings and he didn't return them? That would hurt worse than if Harris Mowery had plunged that knife into her heart.

Chapter Twenty-Three

She wasn't going to answer him. Jared couldn't blame her. He had put her on the spot. She looked as if she wanted to be anywhere else than standing in that waiting room with him and her sister.

She probably wanted to get back to Alex. She'd been gone a long time.

"Forget it," he said. "You don't have to answer that. I'll take you back to the apartment—back to Alex." Maybe he would hook her up to Alex's lie detector test and ask her again. Then he would know if she told him the truth.

"So I can pack?" she asked. "So Alex and I can leave."

And he realized why she hadn't answered her sister's question. Because she wasn't sure how he felt. Because he'd never told her.

"I don't want you to leave," he said. "Ever…"

Then she was in his arms, clutching him closely. "Are you really okay?" she asked.

"Yes." They'd given him some painkillers that

had dulled the ache in his head and his shoulder. But the narcotics had done nothing for his heart—only she could fix that.

"Are you sure you should be checking yourself out?" she asked anxiously.

"I'm fine," he replied, but it was a lie. "At least I will be once you tell me how you feel. Do you want to pack up and leave?"

She shook her head. "No," she replied. "I don't want to leave. Ever…"

Warmth and relief flooded his heart. Her admission made him feel much better than the painkillers had. "That's good," he said as he ignored his wounded shoulder and clutched her closer. "Because I'm never going to let you go again. I love you, Becca."

He didn't care that he'd announced it in front of her sister and his fellow agents who'd joined them in the waiting room—probably when they hadn't been able to find him in the ER.

"I love you," she said. "I've always loved you."

"I know," he said. "I shouldn't have doubted you six years ago." But he'd been scared. He hadn't wanted to put his heart on the line if her feelings hadn't been real. And even if they'd been real, he'd doubted they would have lasted through her disappointment in his being unable to find her sister's killer.

"I should have told you about Alex," she said

as she pulled back. "We've both made mistakes. We've both hurt each other."

He nodded. "But we have the rest of our lives to make it up to each other." He dropped to one knee right there in the waiting room. And he pulled out a jeweler's box. He'd bought the ring the day before. He hadn't had time to get it sized. It probably wouldn't fit. Maybe she wouldn't even like it. But he'd wanted to have the ring for this moment—for when the killer was caught— and it would be safe to propose. He opened the box and held it out to her. "Will you marry me, Becca? Will you become my wife?"

She said nothing; she just stood there, staring at him like she'd been staring at Lexi when he'd kicked open the door to the bride's dressing room. As if she couldn't believe her eyes. "Are you serious?" she asked.

"You can hook me up to Alex's lie detector test and ask me again," he offered with a chuckle. "But yes, I'm serious."

Her eyes widened in surprise.

"I guess I'm an old-fashioned guy," he admitted. "I don't want you to live with me forever without making this official. And as I understand it, we already have a license and a wedding all planned out."

"For a fake wedding…"

He shook his head. "Let's make it real, Becca," he urged her. "Say yes. Become my wife."

"Yes," she said. Then she shouted, "Yes! I want to marry you. I want to become your wife! I love you!"

He slid the ring on her finger, and to his surprise, it fit. Perfectly. Just like the two of them. He pulled her into his arms—where she fit perfectly. Just days ago he'd been dreading everything about their fake wedding. Now he couldn't wait to get to the altar.

PENNY PAYNE WAS RIGHT. The wedding she'd helped Rebecca plan was perfect. But it wasn't because of the beautiful flowers or the dress or the double chocolate cake that Alex and his father couldn't wait to eat. It was because of the people.

Not everybody was there, though. Rebecca's parents had not been as forgiving of Lexi as she and Jared had been. They didn't understand that she would have died had she not played dead. Rebecca couldn't be happier that her sister was alive and able to be her matron of honor. And Alex had two flower girls to walk down the aisle—one on each arm. Becky was blonde and blue-eyed like him while Amanda had her father's fiery-red hair.

And since Rebecca's father wasn't there to walk her down the aisle, George was doing the honors. She held his arm as he walked her toward the altar—toward her groom. She had always thought of him as her brother. Now he officially was.

She smiled up at him through her veil and mouthed the words *thank you*.

And not just for walking her down the aisle. She had him to thank for Lexi being alive and happy.

Lexi had already made it down the aisle. Her girls leaned against her while Alex had gone to the men's side. He stood between Jared and his best man, Nicholas Rus. She smiled with amusement as she remembered how Dalton Reyes, Blaine Campbell and Ash Stryker had teased the other FBI agent. They'd warned him that whoever stood up as best man was the next agent to make his own trek to the altar.

Nick had laughed as if the idea was preposterous. But it had become true for all of them. She hoped it did for him, too. He intended to stay in River City, Michigan, with the family he'd only recently discovered was his.

Rebecca didn't blame him. She was thrilled with her family. She loved having her sister back and George and her nieces. But the most important part of her family stood before her. Jared and Alex. The two loves of her life.

She stopped next to Jared. He lifted her veil and pressed his lips to hers.

Alex tugged on his pants. "Daddy, you're supposed to wait until the end." He must have remembered that from Dalton's wedding. Of course the little boy forgot nothing.

"She's so beautiful I couldn't wait," Jared said.

Alex smiled. "Mommy is very pretty."

The guests laughed. The church was aglow with warmth and happiness and love. Rebecca had never felt so much love.

Jared held her hands as they repeated vows the minister fed them—about loving each other through sickness and health, good times and bad. Their love had already survived all those things, so she knew they would make it just like Jared had promised: forever.

She slid the gold band on Jared's finger, and he slid a gold band on hers, up against the diamond engagement ring he'd already given her.

"I now pronounce you man and wife," the minister said. "You may kiss your bride…again."

The guests laughed.

But Rebecca was focused on Jared as his handsome face lowered to hers again. He kissed her—reverently and then passionately. Applause burst out in the church.

Mrs. Payne had been right. It was the perfect wedding. And theirs would be the perfect marriage.

* * * * *

LARGER-PRINT BOOKS!
GET 2 FREE LARGER-PRINT NOVELS PLUS
2 FREE GIFTS!

✦HARLEQUIN®

INTRIGUE
BREATHTAKING ROMANTIC SUSPENSE

LARGER-PRINT BOOKS!

GET 2 FREE
LARGER-PRINT NOVELS
PLUS 2 FREE
MYSTERY GIFTS

Love Inspired
SUSPENSE
RIVETING INSPIRATIONAL ROMANCE

Larger-print novels are now available...

YES! Please send me 2 FREE LARGER-PRINT Love Inspired® Suspense novels and my 2 FREE mystery gifts (gifts are worth about $10). After receiving them, if I don't wish to receive any more books, I can return the shipping statement marked "cancel." If I don't cancel, I will receive 4 brand-new novels every month and be billed just $5.49 per book in the U.S. or $5.99 per book in Canada. That's a savings of at least 19% off the cover price. It's quite a bargain! Shipping and handling is just 50¢ per book in the U.S. and 75¢ per book in Canada.* I understand that accepting the 2 free books and gifts places me under no obligation to buy anything. I can always return a shipment and cancel at any time. Even if I never buy another book, the two free books and gifts are mine to keep forever.

110/310 IDN GH6P

Name	(PLEASE PRINT)	

Address		Apt. #

City	State/Prov.	Zip/Postal Code

Signature (if under 18, a parent or guardian must sign)

Mail to the **Reader Service:**
IN U.S.A.: P.O. Box 1867, Buffalo, NY 14240-1867
IN CANADA: P.O. Box 609, Fort Erie, Ontario L2A 5X3

**Are you a current subscriber to Love Inspired® Suspense books
and want to receive the larger-print edition?
Call 1-800-873-8635 or visit www.ReaderService.com.**

* Terms and prices subject to change without notice. Prices do not include applicable taxes. Sales tax applicable in N.Y. Canadian residents will be charged applicable taxes. Offer not valid in Quebec. This offer is limited to one order per household. Not valid for current subscribers to Love Inspired Suspense larger-print books. All orders subject to credit approval. Credit or debit balances in a customer's account(s) may be offset by any other outstanding balance owed by or to the customer. Please allow 4 to 6 weeks for delivery. Offer available while quantities last.

Your Privacy—The Reader Service is committed to protecting your privacy. Our Privacy Policy is available online at www.ReaderService.com or upon request from the Reader Service.

We make a portion of our mailing list available to reputable third parties that offer products we believe may interest you. If you prefer that we not exchange your name with third parties, or if you wish to clarify or modify your communication preferences, please visit us at www.ReaderService.com/consumerschoice or write to us at Reader Service Preference Service, P.O. Box 9062, Buffalo, NY 14240-9062. Include your complete name and address.

LISLP15

READERSERVICE.COM

Manage your account online!

- Review your order history
- Manage your payments
- Update your address

*We've designed the
Reader Service website
just for you.*

Enjoy all the features!

- Discover new series available to you, and read excerpts from any series.
- Respond to mailings and special monthly offers.
- Connect with favorite authors at the blog.
- Browse the Bonus Bucks catalog and online-only exculsives.
- Share your feedback.

Visit us at:
ReaderService.com